The Diary
OF
Dolly Makepeace

The Diary

OF

Dolly Makepeace

A Novel By Arthur H. Veasey III

TO: Lisa

Arthur H Veasey III

Jan 28 2013

Copyright © 2011 by Arthur H. Veasey III

This book is a work of fiction. Names, characters, places and incidents are either products of the author's imagination or used fictitiously. Any resemblance to actual events, locales, or persons, living or dead, is purely coincidental. All rights reserved. No part of this publication can be reproduced or transmitted in any form or by any means, electronic or mechanical, without permission in writing from the author or publisher.

Cover design by Sylenda Graf

Edition © 2012

Contents

Haverhill, Massachusetts

Little River

Sinkholes

Long Hill

The Englishman

The Crypt

Fire in the Hole

The Pediment

About The Author

Haverhill, Massachusetts

Dee Dearborn descended the hill to the open meadow below the old house. The property with twenty-five acres of rocky New England soil had been in her family for seven generations, but now that her grandfather had died and with few family members in the area, the land and enduring saltbox would likely go to auction. The river here was tidal, unlike those that emptied into the Great Lake at home in western Michigan. Along this waterway that the Indians called Merrimack, trees sparsely bordered the riverbank, where red-tailed hawks observed the route to the family burial plot above the floodplain.

The grass was wet and ankle high when Dee entered the fieldstone enclave through a rusty iron gate. She counted nineteen gravestones with names etched in sandstone, slate, or granite, several with grotesque death symbols carved into the surface. Winter frost heaves had pushed many backward, some at severe angles, and wind or snow had worn at the engraved lettering. There was no elaborate landscaping, yet the grounds did not seem neglected.

Dutch clover was abundant and wild lilac bushes crowded one end of the plot, lending a feeling of privacy. Dee was fascinated by this ancient connection to her past, as there was nothing like this in Grand Rapids.

She was examining every marker with curiosity and awe, when she came to an abrupt halt. A small dark headstone sat in the shade of a pine tree with a legend that startled her: "Here lies the body of Dolly Makepeace wife of Captain Samuel Dearborn who departed this life Nov 17th 1817 AE 77." Next to it was the headstone of the departed Samuel. The rest of his inscription could not be made out, faded away by generations of New England winters.

Dee was enthralled. This was the grave of an ancestor buried almost two hundred years earlier, with her given name carved in stone. She had been baptized Dolly Dearborn, it was wonderfully alliterative, but her family had shortened it to Dee Dee and the diminutive had stuck.

As she reached out to touch the gravestone, something vaguely familiar struck. A memory, long suppressed, raced in her head. She was eight years old and remanded to her room for being dilatory in her lessons. As she brooded over the punishment a bright figure dressed in white appeared. It told Dee to lie down and close her eyes and that everything would be fine. Dee did exactly as she was asked, because the figure was kind and beautiful. The next morning Dee raced to school where, at ten o'clock, the third and fourth graders assembled for the regional spelling bee contest. Improbably Dee answered every question correctly. When her astonished parents asked how she had become so remarkably proficient she replied: "Dolly Makepeace helped me." The visions persisted intermittently until her teenage years, when gradually they disappeared. Her parents thought she had simply outgrown a childhood fixation. So had she, until now.

Arthur Dearborn mixed a manhattan cocktail for himself, as had been his habit with friends and family for at least the last twenty years. It was a civilized way to begin the dinner hour and a chance to relax and chat with guests. Tonight he would enjoy the company of his niece, who had traveled east for his father's memorial service.

"So, how did you like the farm?"

"It doesn't look like much of a farm, Uncle Arthur," Dee chided.

"Well, you're right. It's not a real working farm anymore, and it hasn't been since my grandfather died, but Father did grow a few Christmas trees and plant strawberries and pumpkins, and that way he got to keep it on the tax rolls as a farm and hold the developers at bay."

"It has been so long since I was last here. I had forgotten the charm of this old house, with its low ceilings and narrow hallways," Dee remarked. "It's like a time warp, a page out of 1776."

"Actually, it was built around 1750 by Thomas Hoadley, who was a brother to Sally Dearborn. Thomas never married, deeded it to Sally's oldest son, Samuel, and it's been occupied by a Dearborn ever since."

"I saw a marker for Samuel Dearborn in the old burial ground. Is that the same one?" Dee asked.

"The one and only—he was the excuse for your grandmother's membership in the DAR. Samuel was a minuteman and a pensioner of the Revolution. You can find a lot of information about his service to Haverhill at the library."

"And what of the grave to his left, Dolly Makepeace?"

"I don't know too much, other than she was married to Samuel. Unfortunately, Americans in those days did not always show proper appreciation for the contributions of our female ancestors, so very little was written down. I do know for a fact that she was the widow of the local minister before she married into the Dearborn clan."

Dee was more than just intrigued by the prospect of researching her family. The discovery of the headstone and the nascent consciousness it stirred, unleashed a rush of emotional energy. For the next several days she pored through records from the First Parish Church, as well as the Special Collections room at the library. Another day she drove to Boston, to the New England Historical Society, where she found excellent resources for information about Captain Dearborn's military service but nothing about Dolly.

On her last night before she would return home to Michigan Dee relaxed alone, reading quietly in the front room that peered across the river. It was late, but she thought she should let the embers burn down before turning in. She leaned over the hearth and stoked the fire, when a noise startled her. Something had fallen and hit the planked floor with a distinct *thud*. She glanced over to where the sound had emanated from and spied something near the carpet, below the built-in shelves.

Carefully returning the fire screen, she stepped through the narrow space of the living room. The object, a small book, lay splayed open, its spine facing upward. It seemed odd that this one volume should have been displaced suddenly from its spot among the hundred others that were lined up along the knotty-pine ledges. There was no one else here. No cats, no Uncle Arthur, no Dearborn ghosts, she said to herself, just to assuage the unnerved feelings that swished inside her stomach.

Finally she reached down and grasped the cause of the disquieting interruption. It was compact, reddish, and leather bound, about an inch thick. The head cap and top were covered with dust but the covers were shiny clean, no doubt from the protection of many years of undisturbed rest between two other, unpopular tomes. On the front, the title read plainly: Line-A-Day. Dee rubbed two fingers gently across the raised gold letters before delicately opening the cover. As she turned the flyleaf, her heart skipped. The inscription, in the handwriting of its owner, jumped off the page: "Dolly Makepeace."

All at once and in a single exhilarating instant, Dee understood what she held in her hand: a diary, a living journal belonging to the enigmatic Dolly, whose life she sought so desperately to uncover. This book could reveal the thoughts, the aspirations—indeed, the emotions—of the woman who had blazed a trail for all Dearborn females more than two centuries earlier. Dee was dizzy with excitement.

September 10, 1774 — Sunny and mild. Apple harvest has begun. Went with the ladies to the orchard behind Jacob Whooley's and gathered a bushel. There is a sense of urgency in the air as talk of separation from England spreads. In the village our minutemen are back on the common, preparing for war. An artist visited the parsonage looking for Asa. His name is Paul Gallimet. It was odd to see this diminutive Frenchman in our town in the midst of such activity.

The parsonage sat high on a hill that gave Dolly a full view of the village, all the way to the river and beyond. Haverhill was now a town of some distinction, the twenty-seventh English settlement in the New World, with a reputation for progressive boldness not found in places like Salem, Weymouth, or Braintree. Taverns like the Freemason's Arm at Harrod's were lively meeting places among the wooden buildings that stood shoulder to shoulder along narrow streets and random pathways. Seven hills guarded the village from the north, and to the south the Merrimack, with its wharves and commercial trade, provided a steady stream of goods and access to the Atlantic.

As early as 1765, town meetings were agitating about excise taxes being imposed on tea and coffee, but a cause of more recent unrest was an act relating to the preservation of "the King's Woods." To the disadvantage of local sawmills, The Royal Navy was using the act to seize trees and timber in northern New England for its own purposes. Extensive timber traced from Long Hill all the way into New Hampshire, and the citizens here did not take kindly to the idea of the British encroaching on their forests. Plus, there were the sinkholes to worry about; if Englishmen were prowling the woods, they might stumble upon the sinkholes, and that was one intrusion the inhabitants of Haverhill would not allow.

Just beyond the porch and across the main road, the common served as a training field where the local militia conducted exercises to provide for the defense and public safety of the town. Of these men, one-third were minutemen, a highly select and mobile force that could be deployed to engage the British on a moment's notice. This was Sam Dearborn's company numbering 115, each man equipped with musket, bayonet, powder, and flints. They drilled for an hour just before sunset three days a week. The purpose of the exercise was to instill discipline in the unit so that a commander or noncommissioned officer could move his troops in a precise, orderly manner in the face of armed conflict with the enemy.

Dolly watched the activity from her drawing room with muted interest. She had been able to powder and cock a musket as well as any man when she was a girl growing up on the marshes. She had been tomboyish and a hell-raiser until the day she married James Makepeace, a descendent of one of the early settlers of Haverhill. That had been an unfortunate union of convenience and one that she had quietly regretted, before his sudden demise had released her from her vows.

After an appropriate bereavement, she had been once again fair game and a fetching widow. Dolly knew that she was a temptation to married men, and so she avoided them on social occasions, cognizant of both the attraction and the resentment she might stir. Yet at age twenty-five, she had found that eligible male candidates were fewer and all too often eccentric.

There had been Jabez Hale, owner of the manufactory on the Little River, who was awkward and shy. She had neatly deflected his attentions by recruiting a love-starved maiden of some aging desperation to redirect his ardent spirit. Daniel Swan was coarse and a bully and she had adroitly avoided his intentions. Asa Pike, however, seemed like safe ground. Harvard-educated and the son of Nathaniel Pike, an esteemed minister of the Church of England, he was scholarly, refined, and good company. He was a member of Haverhill's First Parish when a disagreement subverted the congregation, and he adeptly positioned himself between the two factions to be appointed minister. He was an opportunist, but not in a devious way, and in the balance of all things a man of good character. Although he was almost fifteen years her senior, Dolly made the decision to wed and age gracefully with this genteel partner.

As she thought about the disruption of a war with England, a knocking startled her thoughts back to the present. Walking through the foyer and past her husband's study, she opened the door, half expecting to see one of the ladies from the alms guild. Instead an odd-looking man whom she had never laid eyes on stood before her. He was a sturdy fellow, much shorter than she—about five feet tall, she guessed. His face was a map of tiny blood vessels that culminated in his cheeks. He wore a gentleman's waistcoat under an open frock, and tan breeches that extended to the knees, where they were met by stockings and low-heeled shoes with buckles of the style worn by the French. The stranger cleared his throat.

"*Excusez-moi*, mademoiselle, I am here to call upon the reverend Asa Pike."

"Sir, you have the advantage," she said politely. "May I ask who is calling?"

"*Mais oui*—Paul Gallimet," he replied, removing his hat and bowing deeply at the waist.

"Please come in and sit for a moment. Parson Pike is not here, and I am afraid I do not know when to expect him."

The stranger clasped his hands in a show of appreciation, then made himself at home. Dolly noticed that his fingers were soiled, though not like a blacksmith's, neither were they callused like the hands of a farmer. A colorful pigment highlighted the fingernails, and thumbprints smudged his smock. She wondered if he was an itinerant artist.

Dolly disappeared briefly, returning with a pot of tea and sweet biscuits—not much of a repast, but the best that she could spare with the protests on trade importation making English niceties scarce. Pouring out two servings, she gave her guest a gentle but curious look.

"May I ask what your business is with my husband, monsieur?"

Gallimet's nose wrinkled above his teacup in response. "We live in a changing world, *n'est-ce pas*? I am here to capture the realism and pragmatism of America by oil on canvas."

Dolly was bemused. "And someone has commissioned these works?"

"No, no, I create portraits, a few landscapes, and hope for some notice and patronage."

"What does Parson Pike have to do with all of this?"

"I wish to paint his portrait, madame, as well as the portraits of other important men. Such honorable subjects will serve as testimony to my skill."

Now bemusement turned to suspicion. "How did you come to arrive here, monsieur?"

Gallimet wet his lips before responding wistfully, "I fled France with the Huguenots, first to New York and now New England, where I intend to establish myself as *un artiste de peinture*."

"And do you have references?"

"*Non*, I am so new to your country, madame, but I was apprenticed in Paris to François Boucher."

His words caught Dolly off guard. A book about famous European painters that her friend Amy Greenleaf had shared with her from her father's library had captivated Dolly as a young girl. Among the artists portrayed, Boucher was as prolific as any, with important works disseminated throughout Europe.

"And where would this sitting be?" Dolly inquired.

"At Harrod's, madame. I have a studio with morning sun and favorable terms."

Asa Pike was an early riser, and on Saturday he was at work sermonizing in his study. This was the act of saying aloud his Sunday homily before a mirror so that he could practice facial expressions to match the Lord's message. Dolly waited until the rehearsal was done to recount the French painter's visit and the proposed sitting, as Asa tried to contain his elation.

"This is wonderful news, my dear. A portrait is a true measure of a gentleman's standing among the most learned and admired men of the colonies. Why, Parson Wibird will be steeped in envy." As he spoke, through the window he could see the minutemen on parade, with their young captain in command. He frowned for a moment, then repaired the smile as he faced Dolly again. "What splendid news; you must learn the details of my preparation."

Sam was instructing his company in military drill, when he noticed the man with his easel, canvas, and palette near the northeast corner of the common. Normally onlookers did not catch his eye, but the little artist was an odd figure and a slight distraction to Dearborn, if not to his men.

When retreat sounded, he approached the intruder with a flat greeting.

"Good afternoon, I'm Captain Dearborn of the Twenty-first Massachusetts Militia and Minutemen."

The Frenchman was chirpy. "Ah, Captain, your reputation precedes you. I am Gallimet, a humble artist in admiration of your obvious command of military tactics. I hope to capture the devotion and bravery of you and your men on my canvas, but I fear that will be a difficult task."

"Yes," said Dearborn, "especially when we have not yet held ourselves accountable to the English."

"*Fils de la Liberte*—the Redcoats will be startled by your resolve, I have little doubt," Gallimet chuckled. "But of course," he whispered facetiously, "my neutrality precludes me from taking sides."

Spoken like a Frenchman, Sam thought as he retreated to the parade ground.

"Captain!" Gallimet called. "I would like a sitting with you, dress uniform, blue coat, turned up with buff, and gold buttons, just like Washington."

Harrod's was a two-story building, low-posted and rambling over much ground, with numerous small windows, a front porch, and a long shed attached for horses and vehicles. It had never been painted, but time had turned it a deep, rich brown. Elizabeth Hartshorne was the hostess, and she kept a neat hostelry. Two dollars per week was the price of a room, but Gallimet had bargained her down to one dollar and the promise of a painting of the village, which would be a lovely attraction for the patrons at the Freemason's Arm. The room on the second floor was airy and had a sunny exposure. From its windows one could see the common to the left, the parsonage just above, and the sweep of the Merrimack to the right. An easel that reached from floor to ceiling stood at one end of the room; rows of empty canvases leaned against the wall.

"Mr. Gallimet," Elizabeth Hartshorne called from the head of the long hallway, "you have a visitor: Mrs. Makepeace to see you."

For some reason, no one had ever stopped calling Dolly Mrs. Makepeace, and she did not object. Even Asa had taken to calling her "my bride, the good Mrs. Makepeace" when referring to her in conversation with the members of his congregation. Today she was on a small mission to discuss her husband's portrait.

"Monsieur, I am here to arrange the details of the portrait sitting for Parson Pike."

The artist gave a short-hand gesture that signaled consent. Dolly's eyes inspected the rag-strewn room, with its pungent smell of linseed oil and paint. Gallimet was wiping a brush and spoke rapidly without looking at her.

"Madame, he must wear the ecclesiastical vestments that characterize high position in the clergy. I suggest a white linen cravat and full academic gown. He will hold in his hand a King James English-version Bible. The background should combine color and motif that one would associate with scholarship. I suggest purple with Ionic columns. Do you have any questions?"

Dolly was dumbfounded. "When will you start?" she asked.

Gallimet smiled. "This will all be achieved, madame, but first I must finish what I have started."

Started? What could that mean? Gallimet had been in Haverhill for barely a fortnight; what could take precedence over her husband, the right Reverend Pike?

"May I see?" she half demanded.

The Frenchman arched his brow as if to signal disapproval, but then removed a drape from the canvas before him to reveal the incomplete likeness of a colonial militiaman with rifle raised chest high, wearing a waistcoat, breeches, and gray stockings with half boots and gaiters.

Dolly's stare was incredulous. The countenance was not yet painted, but she knew immediately who this figure must be and she felt a blush of inescapable excitement.

Long Hill rose gradually above the Little River. It was about one mile long and half or three-quarters of a mile wide. There were sloping meadows on both sides and timber at the top. Just below the tree line were five ancient sinkholes. Three were shallow but wide enough to swallow an inattentive traveler making his way at night. The other two extended deep into the side of the hill, where narrow entrances led to an expansive network of caves. Legend had it that the Indians had used them as burial grounds, but no remains had ever been found.

What the caves did contain was a seemingly unlimited supply of saltpeter. Also called potassium nitrate, saltpeter was a naturally occurring mineral deposit that formed on cave walls and was a critical oxidizing component of gunpowder. This local load produced a particularly powerful yet stable mixture that the powdermakers considered safer to manufacture and the riflemen found easier to load and fire.

Most of the inhabitants of Haverhill had known of the caves' existence since the Indian uprisings but had kept the remote location a secret from outsiders. Now their potential to sustain the production of superior ammunition made them an extremely strategic resource in the event of open revolt against the British.

The man responsible for the covert operation was Colonel Thomas Rollins. Rollins was a veteran Indian fighter, having waged numerous wilderness assaults against the French and their native allies during the Seven Years War. At age sixty, he was now the senior officer of the colonial regulars who were mustered from Andover to Haverhill. On this day, Rollins had summoned Sam to Long Hill. Neither man was in uniform, and they passed easily for ordinary journeymen as their horses labored up the incline to the mining operation.

Rollins spoke in a voice that was calm but imperative. "Two days ago British soldiers removed two hundred fifty half barrels from the Powder House at Cambridge, and another detachment carried off two small cannons. Four thousand men assembled on the common in protest, until grenadiers fired shots into the air to intimidate them. Rumors of war are widespread, Sam. I'm leaving tomorrow to meet with Colonel Prescott. He's worried about munitions, and I'm sure he will ask me for assurances that the British will not find our sinkholes."

Sam knew this was tricky. The sinkhole operations weren't openly discussed, but there they were in easy view if you went looking for them.

"There's more, Sam: someone has been stealing powder from our operation. Not large stores all at once, but a keg here, a rundlet there. It all adds up."

"So our thief could be someone working at the mine," Sam said.

"Or someone with access, like a teamster moving contraband," Rollins acknowledged.

Two plain wooden structures erected just below the sinkholes on Little River served as production mills where charcoal, sulfur, and saltpeter were ground separately, then mixed together in the complex and dangerous process that created gunpowder. Ephraim Merrill was the man in charge of production. Several explosions in the early years had made him cautious and painstaking in his supervision.

As they entered the center of the facility Rollins shouted above the din: "Ephraim!"

Merrill gave the colonel a nod.

"Ephraim, I leave for Charlestown tomorrow. Colonel Prescott will want to discuss capacity."

"We can deliver two hundred barrels a month, and that's working 'round the clock, Colonel."

"He's going to ask for more, Ephraim."

"Colonel, even if we could do it, we don't have enough coopers in the village to stave the barrels."

"I can arrange for more barrels from Amesbury," Sam countered. Merrill scowled.

"It's a dangerous undertaking, pushing the men to the limit."

"That's why we have recruited the expert, Ephraim. He will instruct your powdermakers in the newest processes."

"I think it's a big risk bringing in a new man, Colonel."

"But a necessary one, Ephraim, one that our cause may depend upon in the days and months ahead."

Rollins knew the dangers. Gunpowder was safe when mixed in small quantities, but in large production facilities like this, the slightest misstep could spell disaster.

As the two men rode back to the village, Sam was immersed in thought. The sinkholes had to be mined efficiently and protected at all costs if the Americans were to have any chance in a war with the British. The mine was a well-guarded secret, yet he was troubled. Who could be pilfering gunpowder, and who was this expert? Colonel Rollins would not reveal the names of an agent even to him, but any breach of confidence could bring the British into the valley in direct confrontation with his minutemen. There were too many uncertain loyalties, he thought.

"What do you think of our pacifist friend?" Sam asked.

"If you mean Asa Pike, I don't know where his allegiance resides," Rollins answered. "He is a Congregationalist, so the Church of England does not bind him to the crown like his father, who was a Tory till the day he died. In any event, I would keep an eye on him."

Boston and Cambridge were rife with Tories and spies. In settlements farther out, a man's conscience was fairly known to his neighbor. Jacob Whooley, who lived on the Bradford side of the river in a large house overlooking the ferry, might be partial to King George III, but he declared himself neutral. Most in Haverhill were sympathetic to the cause, if not outright patriots. Sam believed that the secret of the sinkholes was safe among them. But Asa Pike was an intellectual who preached nonviolence, and he seemed disposed to trust the British. Of Gallimet, Sam knew nothing. And then there were the Swan men. They were "skinners" who pledged no loyalty to either side. For now, he decided, he would pay his respects to the good Parson Pike.

September 15, 1774 — Mostly sunny and breezy, mercury at 65. Captain Dearborn stopped by hoping to find Parson Pike. He stayed for tea and we had a splendid conversation that has aroused my curiosity. Asa took a mare out early and rode to the West Parish—arrived back around five o'clock in a tiff. Something is afoot.

The congregation of the First Parish had built the parsonage the year before, and it was as fine a residence as any in Haverhill. It had two stories and a large front entrance with two windows on each side that boasted glass panes of six over six. Five more windows fronted the second floor, with four columns supporting a pediment in perfect symmetry. Sam ascended the front steps smartly and knocked twice. Moments later he heard quick footsteps and Dolly appeared at the doorway.

"Captain Dearborn, what a pleasure. Please come in."

Sam stepped into the foyer. To his right he could see an elegant drawing room with a conspicuous silver service surrounded by English furniture in the William and Mary style. He glanced toward the minister's study opposite. "I was hoping to find your husband at home."

"Oh, I am sorry; Asa left early this morning to visit one of his lost sheep, as he likes to call them, a parishioner who has been absent from the meetinghouse for more than a month of Sundays. Will you sit and take a cup of tea with me?"

"Thank you, I would like that."

"It has been some time since I have had such distinguished company, Captain."

"The pleasure is mine. You have a beautiful home here, elegantly appointed."

"You are obviously a man of excellent taste, Captain," Dolly smiled. "Now, what can our parish do to forge an active and mutually supportive allegiance with our minutemen?"

"I was hoping to prevail upon Asa to depart from the usual religious theme this Sunday and speak to the duty of Christian men to fight for liberty against tyranny."

"It seems like an unusual thing to address such an important public issue from the pulpit. I would think the pamphleteers a more practical voice."

"For a larger audience, perhaps, but our neighbors regard the meetinghouse as a forum of convenience for such discussion."

"Then I will be more than pleased to communicate your request to Parson Pike."

"It will strengthen resolve among my men to find Providence in their favor, thank you."

"I must say, Captain, I have observed your field exercises on the common; there is a sharpness to your men that is admirable."

"So you have an eye for military drill. I am surprised—I would have thought your sentiments to be more like those of the Friends."

"Quakers? Hardly, Captain. I subscribe to my own political views." Sam could not resist a mischievous repartee.

"That is a bold outlook in this day and age, Mrs. Makepeace. I would have thought time spent debating such opinions to be outside the boundaries of female gossip."

"Women should not be content with the roles assigned by society; we are not just pretty faces, we have the intellect to think and act as well as any man."

"And where does that leave all the pretty faces?"

"The prettiest girl can give only what she has, Captain."

Until now, Sam had suppressed his attraction to Dolly. She was self-educated and striking in appearance and had a mind of her own. He had devoted little time to chasing the younger females in town, since he was absorbed in his military training and generally distracted by the clouds of war. Yet Dolly possessed ideal qualities that he found appealing—scandalous thoughts, he realized: she was the wife of his minister.

The pleasantness of their company lingered until propriety dictated that it was time to part. As Sam was leaving, he noticed Asa Pike's chaise inside the carriage house. "I thought the parson was making calls," he said absently.

"He is, but Ephraim Merrill lives out in the West Parish. The roads were washed out last week, so he went on horseback."

If Sam tried to conceal his alarm at the disclosure, it was not enough to escape Dolly. He was stoic yet clearly daunted by the news, and she could sense that concern.

"Good day, Mrs. Makepeace."

Asa was never comfortable on horseback, nor could he get used to the pounding in the stirrups as his tall gray mare clamored down the soggy hillside. She kept slipping and snorting, her head thrusting back and forth, so that he had to lean way back in the saddle in order to maintain his center of gravity and keep from slipping off. Finally he reached a point where the meadow leveled, and the mare went into an easy lope.

Haverhill was a consolation of sorts to Asa. He would have preferred a ministry in Cambridge or Salem, but there were too many scholars and not enough pulpits to go around. Despite his Harvard pedigree, he was shy and his oratory skills had paled when he competed for the important places where serious preaching was done. To bide his time, he had found a teaching position in Haverhill and had been a boarder at Benjamin Greenleaf's household, where he met Dolly. She was a frequent visitor and possessed a bearing and a lively, cheerful disposition that he envied. Though he was charmed and his admiration was genuine, he felt no longing for true intimacy and showed Dolly no real tenderness of affection, and she sensed his reticence. Therefore, she was surprised after James Makepeace died that Asa asked for her hand.

He was prompt because he knew other suitors were in the hunt, yet when she accepted his proposal he was wholly unprepared, as if matrimony were one of life's mysteries that had never held his attention. The union was advantageous, however, and a ministry followed soon after their wedding. Asa enjoyed a generous dowry and had found intellectual stimulation with someone he adored; yet deep down in his gut, where instincts should have been aroused, he harbored doubts that his carnal obligations to his bride could be sustained.

Asa could see in the distance the place where Ephraim Merrill lived and toiled when he wasn't at home in the village. An old shack fronted the two larger wooden structures that were close to the stream. Asa dismounted the mare and tied her to an old hitching post. Knocking on the door, he called Merrill's name. There was no answer, so he raised the latch and peered in through the shack's darkened doorway. Traces of fresh coffee sat on top of an old stove, so Asa decided to investigate the two larger buildings identified with hand-painted signs: Building No. 1 and Building No. 2.

As he neared Building No. 1, he could hear sounds much like those of a gristmill. The door was open, so he stepped inside, his eyes needing a minute to adjust from the sunlight outdoors to within the darkened, windowless structure. He shouted Merrill's name, but the squeaking and grinding noises drowned him out.

He spotted a faint light and shadows at the other end of the room. He approached cautiously to avoid tripping over the cast-iron vats and wooden barrels scattered around him. A half-opened doorway was visible just ahead. Inside Ephraim Merrill was bent over a makeshift table with large entry journals spread before him, as well as another figure whom Asa thought familiar but whom he could not immediately recognize, as the man's back was turned three quarters away from Asa's line of vision. Asa was about to speak up when, without warning, a small explosion shook the walls around them. The two men stood up and scrambled around the table and through the doorway beyond. As the second man turned, Asa saw his face clearly. It was the Frenchman Paul Gallimet.

Asa stepped quickly into the vacated room. On the desk sat the journals, with entries like none he had seen before: formulas similar to those he remembered from the study halls of the chemists at Harvard. As he searched for a list of compounds, two words leaped out at him: "black powder." He turned the pages fast enough to discover that enormous quantities of explosives were being produced and transferred to powder houses as far away as Albany and Worcester.

Asa was bewildered. This was a massive operation that could only feed the flames of rebellion. He returned the journals to their original page positions and retreated silently. Outside again, he stared at the buildings. Smoke and dust were emanating from Building No. 2, but no real damage was apparent. He mounted the mare and started back to the village.

Thomas Rollins and William Prescott respected each other. Both men had served in the earlier conflict with France and had earned the rank of colonel by way of experience, knowledge, and bravery. Tonight they met in secrecy at a tavern in Charlestown. The pub was small and crowded as the two men conversed amid laughter, several arguments, and the smoke from a dozen or so tobacco pipes.

"The British are intent on impounding all of our munitions, Thomas. It is imperative that your sinkholes achieve maximum production, and soon."

"The French chemist has arrived under guise and he is already making changes to improve the quality of the powder and increase output to three hundred barrels per month."

"Good," Prescott replied. "And what about distribution?"

"We have assembled an armory in Andover to serve as a distribution point. That way, even if the barrels are discovered, our source of production will remain a secret and we will simply organize a new supply center."

Prescott nodded in satisfaction. "Whom have you entrusted to oversee the secrecy and security of the mission?"

"I plan to recruit Sam Dearborn."

"I thought he was a minuteman."

"He is, but I have asked for his release to the militia."

"You may get some resistance. He doesn't much care for the French or the English, and he yearns for the pitch of battle to honor his father's memory. If he stands his ground it's only because he longs for the good fight, Thomas."

Rollins knew that if open warfare broke out he would have to release Sam to lead his company of minutemen, but in the time leading up to outright rebellion, he meant to get the most out of his intelligent planning and organizational skills. "He's a good man and we can count on him, William." It was late and he knew he had given Prescott the reassurance he needed, so he prepared to depart.

"Thomas," Prescott warned, "you need to stay very alert. The rumor mill professes a spy out there who calls himself Kestrel. He supposedly supplies the British with information in exchange for exorbitant goods like linen, cut glass, and fine wines."

"Well, that's a new one, Colonel. I daresay the French are not so rapacious as this bird of prey."

When Rollins returned and heard about the explosion at Building No. 2, he was relieved to learn that no one had been hurt. A mixture left unattended to dry had accidentally ignited, causing a good deal of smoke but little damage. Ephraim Merrill had come to town for provisions and figured he'd better report the incident.

"It took us the better part of the day cleaning up," Ephraim said, "but we're back on schedule."

"And how is the chemist?" Rollins asked.

"It took a little bit of the boast out of him, but otherwise he is back to the alchemy."

"I'm asking Sam to be responsible for the security of the mill and for the safe movement of munitions to Andover from here on out. I plan to inform him about the Frenchman."

"You sure he doesn't already know?"

"No, why?"

"Well, that's interesting, because somebody was there investigating. I found fresh hoof marks at the shack after the accident. I just assumed it was Dearborn."

When Asa Pike returned to town he stabled the mare and hastened to his study. He dislodged Ames' Almanack from his bookshelf and thumbed through it, looking for a piece that he remembered about explosives. The dissertation was brief, but what he ascertained was that the French had advanced the techniques of munitions production and were more than happy to share their practices with England's adversaries.

At that instant, Dolly entered the room. "Asa, you are back sooner than I expected." Asa looked at Dolly quizzically.

"When did the artist say he would begin the sitting for my portrait?"

"He did not name a date."

"Has anyone seen any of his paintings? To have some appreciation of his talent, that is?"

"Well, I viewed one portrait that was in progress. Why do you ask?"

"No reason. I am just curious. I have another call to make, my dear, but I will be back in time for supper."

Asa entered Harrod's through the side door opposite the common. Mrs. Hartshorne was busy sweeping the floors in the tavern room, so he slipped unnoticed up the flight of stairs to the second floor. He found the room where Gallimet kept his studio and entered quietly. Tools of the artist's trade were positioned around the room but were uniformly clean, with little sign of activity. On the easel was a canvas draped with a cloth—the work that Dolly had seen, he guessed. He raised the cover to reveal the unfinished portrait of a military man, a soldier with no face. He looked closer and noticed something odd. Oil paints took a long time to set and usually retained a degree of tackiness for some period of time. This portrait was dry to the touch. He looked around the room to see if there was another canvas that might be a more recent effort. Most of the ones resting against the wall were blank, but one long rectangular canvas resting on its side caught his eye. The top edge was dark with brushstrokes. He lifted it and set it upright against the soldier's portrait and in the sunlight.

Asa was bewildered. There before him was a portrait of a man in the vestments of a cleric: white linen cravat, full academic gown, and holding in his hand a King James English bible. But as with the military portrait, there was no countenance, no features to identify the gentleman in the painting. Nor was the painting recent. The pigment was dry to the touch.

September 18, 1774 — Rainy, windy, and cold. Went down to the wharves in search of my contact whom I sought out for an investigation. The price is dear. This skulduggery with the rabble is most unpleasant yet a necessary peril. These are troublesome times.

Dolly was gardening, when a swallow swooped low through the yard, a sure sign that bad weather was ahead. She placed her hands on both knees in reflection. Sam Dearborn's visit had been unusual enough, but together with Asa's peculiar behavior she was certain something was going on. A sea captain's daughter, she had been taught never to look back once your ship left port, for that would mean you were not ready to brave the seas and complete your voyage. So she changed into a simple dress, a limp garment composed of two lengths of fabric pinch-pleated at the waist, with wide, soft sleeves sewn in at the bodice. A plain outdoor bonnet covered her head and partially obscured her features as she walked down the hill into the rainy wharves along the river. The wharves at night were rumored to be the hangout of harlots, thieves, and even ghosts. Dolly was undeterred, until, as she scampered across the wooden planking, an old merchant ship rubbed against the pilings, creating an eerie sound that caused her to look around nervously for the object of her search.

Bart Preble was a ferryman whose appetite for grog, along with advancing years, had caused him to become shabby and disreputable among his fellow townsmen. Occasionally he would disappear for days, then reappear sober. He labored at the parsonage when odd jobs were required, and Dolly knew him to be sly and coy, yet she also observed that he could be counted on to know or find out most of the secrets that simmered below the surface of the town. Tonight he startled her from behind.

"Ay, missus, what brings ye down here on such a miserable night?" Dolly placed her hand to her mouth to stifle a modest shriek.

"Mr. Preble, if you were a cow I would tie a bell around your neck."

"Sorry, Mrs. Makepeace, I didn't know it was you till you turned and faced me."

Dolly composed herself. "That's all right, that's quite all right, Mr. Preble. I wish to conduct a business transaction, a contract for your services, if you will."

Preble raised an eyebrow. "What kind of a transaction would that be, ma'am?"

Dolly motioned him to the end of the wharf, where she was sure they could not be overheard. "I am in need of information about certain activities that have created some level of intrigue between Parson Pike and Captain Dearborn. I know only that instigators are at play in a situation that could become dangerous if mischievous spies were to claim this to be some sort of treasonous affair."

Preble looked at her with a puzzled expression. "And where does the trail begin, Mrs. Makepeace?"

"The West Parish. Something out there is drawing their attention. And, Mr. Preble, this inquiry has to be handled with utmost discretion."

"And what of my remuneration?"

"Five Spanish dollars now and five more when you have completed the assignment." She handed him a small purse, which he slipped into his belt without looking. "Mr. Preble," Dolly repeated, staring through the rain toward the village, "the Frenchman who has taken residence at Harrod's, I do not know why, but I have misgivings about him. See if he is somehow involved."

In Boston, the British commander Thomas Gage was receiving information that colonists were smuggling more gunpowder and munitions and building up military stock in towns and villages throughout the region. Although he had successfully confiscated several magazine stores in Cambridge and Medford, reports persisted of large supplies of black powder being distributed from somewhere up north. He spoke in an impatient tone to his lieutenant, Hannibal Jones.

"I assume you have agents in the field who can infiltrate these bands of smugglers." Jones was an ambitious young officer anxious to demonstrate his efficient military talents.

"General, I have a number of informants but only one that has both ties to the northern region and the guile to gain access to the upper echelon of the rebel conspirators."

Gage settled back in his chair. "Then why not engage this spymaster at once?"

"The engagement will come at a steep price, General. This agent understands the stakes at play, and as a result his services will be dear."

"I will commit whatever portion of the King's treasure is necessary to assure the destruction of this operation."

"Very well, Sir, I will arrange a meeting for tomorrow night. However, my contact is secretive and cautious and is known to me only as the Kestrel. We have met just a few times in clandestine locations and in the dark, where faces are not revealed."

"The Kestrel," Gage repeated quietly to himself while stroking his chin with a curious approval.

The Kestrel traveled by horseback for approximately nine miles to a small farm just southwest of the Shawsheen River, a small tributary that flowed northward into the Merrimack. There was an old barn there that had seen better days but served as a place to store hay for livestock in winter months. It was isolated enough, but not too far from the Post Road.

In the darkness the agent heard the sound of riders and looked through the barn boards onto a moonlit terrain. Two men in dark cloaks draped over red coats dismounted. As they approached the doorway, the taller one called out expectantly, "Kestrel."

There was no answer, so they stepped inside and began looking for a lantern, when the door closed with a bang from behind. The two men turned on their heels, squinting through the darkness at a lamp with a flame so small that it hardly gave off any illumination beyond three or four feet. At just about that distance and to the left sat the Kestrel, a hooded cloak overshadowing any features.

"Lieutenant Jones, I presume," the Kestrel whispered in a gravel voice.

"Ah, my friend Kestrel," Jones greeted him. "This is Corporal Daggett." The Kestrel nodded. "I am pleased that my inquiry found its way to you so that this meeting could be arranged," he said in a nasal British accent.

"I have traveled some distance and it is late, so please state your business, Lieutenant."

The corporal fidgeted nervously, but Jones responded with a disarming calmness. "Excellent, then—right to the matter at hand, Kestrel. Large stocks of gunpowder are being smuggled into Cambridge, Charlestown, Medford, and beyond. We do not believe the French are supplying these munitions, because Halifax is the nearest port of French entry and our informants tell us there is no activity that would result in such large transfers of explosives. These caches of nitrates are smuggled regularly and with short notice, as far as we can tell. This leads us to believe that their source is located somewhere in the Merrimack Valley. We need you to find out who and where."

"And if I can uncover this information, what will you do with it, Lieutenant? Your British forces are retreating to Boston, I am told, and we are a long way from Boston."

"I am a cavalryman by training, sir, and I have in my command a company of riders who are both efficient and deadly." The nasal accent disappeared as Jones intoned his warning with a fixed glare. The corporal shifted his weight anxiously during the tense moment before the Kestrel responded.

"I have no information of this manufactory, but I will begin an investigation for the right terms, Lieutenant: one hundred pounds of Virginia tobacco, three dozen bottles of Château Margaux, and one chest of British East India Tea."

The corporal swallowed hard and waited for the lieutenant to explode into a tirade. A chest of East India Tea was one thing, but the demands for fine wine and Virginia tobacco were extravagant. But after a pause, Jones replied mildly enough.

"The tea is outside with my mount, as a retainer of good faith, Kestrel. The rest will be delivered to you incrementally, and at such times and places as we shall agree upon, when your information is received and confirmed."

The Kestrel looked up at Jones, the light revealing his features for just an instant. "I accept."

Little River

A hard rain settled in over the Merrimack Valley, causing a rare autumn freshet that swelled every nearby river and stream. The enduring Little River tributary owed its existence to a small pond in southern New Hampshire just over the border. The stream quietly pushed its way past a strip mall; then, unobserved, it flowed beneath Interstate 495 through Haverhill, achieving maximum momentum at the foot of Long Hill before cascading over a rock dam and emptying into the Merrimack.

Just above the shrouded stream on the backside of a cemetery, a gray-haired gentleman turned up the collar of his mackinaw to keep the moisture out, then turned off the fog lamps on his Range Rover. The hard gravel that guided him through the darkness to the portion of the grounds with which he was familiar was solid underfoot. He stepped from the vehicle and walked twenty-one paces to a rectangular tomb. It was a timeworn grave approximately six feet long, three feet wide, and three feet high, with a limestone slab covering a granite vault. As he did on every other visit, he looked over his shoulder to be sure he was alone, then closed his eyes tightly, as if straining under some enormous weight.

A slight tremor shook the ground beneath him, and in his mind's eye lights emanated from every seam in the grave box, casting macabre shadows followed by sounds, a wailing really, one of which beckoned him to a place where he could not go. He desperately wanted to answer the call, but he knew that he did not have the power. Yet on this night, something intervened. He sensed that some spiritual energy, a third eye, was gaining acceptance in the paranormal space that had always been his domain. Someone possessing a clairvoyance stronger than any he had known was channeling the dead, intruding into the immortal soul of his ancestral ghost. He knew instantly that he must locate this person.

September 24, 1774 — Mostly sunny and blustery, mercury 60. Sunday service attracted a larger than usual congregation. Recent events in Boston and Cambridge have put everyone on edge. Asa preaches conciliation, but the men here are of a quarrelsome disposition—my heart lies somewhere between.

The First Parish was a model for New England meetinghouses, with row after row of box pews on the ground floor, flanked by a gallery of smaller pews that overhung the center pulpit where Asa Pike exhorted his congregation. A steeple rose above the south entrance, encasing a brass bell that struck its pitch in brief intervals as it summoned worshipers to service. Large vestibule doors led the way to a broad aisle where pews were assigned by rank, wealth, or whatever else determined a man's standing.

Sam's spot was directly behind that of Colonel Rollins, who sat across from Jacob Whooley. To the left and facing east was the ministerial pew, from which Dolly observed the congregants as they completed the seating order all the way to the back, where Bart Preble occupied humility row.

The service began as it always did, with an invocation followed by a reading of the scriptures, then prayer and more prayer before Asa Pike began his homily. He was always long-winded, and Sam's mind wandered as he waited for Asa to transition his sermon into a resolution for the cause of liberty. He was thinking about the sinkholes, the pilfering, the accidental explosion, and the responsibility for making it all safe from British hands, when Asa's words caught him off guard.

"I shall think of myself the happiest of men if I can, through God's hand, be instrumental in restoring the bonds of friendship between men who, though separated by an ocean, share the same language, religion, and moral confidence."

A bond of friendship was one thing, acts of coercion quite another. Sam wanted to believe that Asa's loyalties were to his neighbors, despite his pacifism, but now he was unsure.

When the service concluded, Sam followed the reception line to where the parson greeted the congregants as they were leaving the meetinghouse.

Asa extended his arm and offered a handshake. "Good day to you, Captain. Always a comfort to have our leading parishioners celebrating the word of God."

Sam was fuming and could barely restrain his response. "Have no doubt as to my strength of faith, Parson; after all, our foes come at us with haughty strides, so whatever grateful offerings we bring, we shall guard with the sword."

"Well said, Captain." Dolly spoke calmly as she stepped to her husband's side. "I can imagine that men of conscience can abide by separate rules of conduct and achieve the same loyal place of honor."

"I believe that most American clergymen have been helpful in building popular support for our grievances against England, madam. I have high regard for those who offer pastoral respect for our cause."

"My admiration for our militia is boundless, Captain," Asa responded pretentiously, before averting his glance to rejoin the procession of congregants. Dolly's attempt at diplomacy was summarily undermined; she cast her eyes downward.

Outside, Colonel Rollins caught Sam's attention and the two men walked casually together to the edge of the common. "Sam, I want to change the protocol. I have a feeling that the route to Andover may have been compromised and your midnight transports could be at risk."

Sam turned his head toward Rollins. "Why? What have you learned?"

"Caleb Bailey was leading his horse from pasture under last week's full moon, when he saw two men on horseback on the Post Road near Shawsheen. Swears they were Redcoats."

Sam's cheeks puffed out as he expelled the air from his lungs. "What do you propose as an alternative?"

Rollins turned his gaze toward the river. "I am suggesting that we load up that old sloop and move our goods at night to Newburyport. Prescott will arrange for another vessel to rendezvous with you to take possession of the powder and smuggle it all the way to Charlestown, right under General Gage's nose."

"That's going to attract a lot of attention on the wharf," Sam remarked.

"Label them rum barrels and load your consignment at night," said Rollins. "Our good merchant Benjamin Davis has agreed to take part in the deception."

The colonel thought of everything, Sam thought. Yet he found the news of British riders at Shawsheen disturbing. He was worried about espionage.

It was a cool night on the river, and Sam watched closely as men arrived with teams of horses and transferred barrels of contraband to the cargo hold of the sloop *Naomi*. This was a much larger load than they usually transported overland, and it took about three hours to secure the makeshift magazine and prepare to get under way at sunrise. From his perch near the head of the gangway, Bart Preble observed the activity and signed on to assist in the transfer. Once in the hold and out of sight, he gave the barrels a close inspection. As a boy he had apprenticed for a cooper, before tiring of the trade. But he had learned enough to know that these were dry-tight casks designed to keep dry goods in and moisture out, definitely not the kind made for spirits or other liquids. Preble counted: there were thirty-six in all.

As the sky brightened, Sam gave orders for all hands to clear the deck. Preble scrambled furtively out of the hold, leaping to the wharf just as deckhands threw off the lines that held the sloop in place. The boatswain pushed the tiller hard to the lee side, until the early-morning breeze filled a single foresail and with a favorable tidal current they began their voyage eastward and downriver.

In spite of many pristine sources, most Americans avoided drinking water, as it was thought to be a sure cause of illness from contamination. As a result, wine, spirits, and especially beer were consumed daily. The Freemason's Arm was the most popular tavern in the town, for its central location. Paul Gallimet hoisted a goblet of Madeira as the tavern buzzed with eager patrons warming themselves by the large fireplace. As he surveyed the crowd, Bart Preble appeared from out of nowhere and collapsed his heavy frame into the chair directly opposite Gallimet.

"Aye, Frenchie, do you mind if I join you?"

"*Mais oui.*" Gallimet eyed the disheveled Preble with some condescension. Bart gave the barmaid a wink and she arrived with a tankard of ale, from which he savored a long but neat sip. He stared at the goblet in the Frenchman's grip.

"How long since you've sipped one of them fancy libations from France?" Bart asked with a friendly smirk.

"Ah, so many seasons have passed in Provence. It is my lot in the colonies to suffer the *vin de* Madère, monsieur, but this cannot be avoided as long as the English continue their embargo."

"Well, I'm no expert, but it seems like this one has a fine bouquet to it," Bart said with a slight song to his voice, reaching nonchalantly into a pack next to his chair. Gallimet glanced at the bottle that emerged, then rubbed his eyes in disbelief.

"Aha, a rosé from the Port of Bandol. The vineyards there are among the oldest in my country. How did you come upon this, monsieur?"

"I have a friend—a client, really—who sometimes pays for my services in kind. A sort of bartering arrangement, you might say."

Gallimet looked at him suspiciously. "And may I ask who this gentleman is and where he resides?"

"The gentleman in question lives a quiet but cultivated existence with his library of books and a vaulted cellar of fine wines the likes of which you could only dream, yet he prefers an inconspicuous lifestyle above social prominence. I cannot reveal his identity without permission."

A wine cellar of French wines was an irresistible passion for Gallimet, but he would need some sort of leverage to gain access. The Frenchman thought for a long, hard moment. A connoisseur and a man of letters would undoubtedly respond to portraiture, if only for private enjoyment. He stared back at Preble. "Monsieur, would you be kind enough to convey my admiration and good wishes to your benefactor? I would honor an introduction to propose a painting of his likeness as a tribute to his sophistication and intellect." The Frenchman passed a small purse under the table, which Bart tucked neatly into his waistband.

No man in the settlement was more prominent than Jacob Whooley. He was a descendant of the Whooley family of Yorkshire, England. His great-grandfather Sir Richard Whooley had come to the New World aboard the ship *Arbella* with governor John Winthrop and settled in Ipswich. His father, Nathaniel, had come to Haverhill in 1720 and built the handsome manor house on the south side of the river where Jacob resided as a bachelor and a gentleman. Jacob was a friendly chap on social occasions and private in his personal affairs, and he had two sustaining interests in life.

First and foremost was heraldry and the trappings of aristocracy—emblems, the family coat of arms, sculpted crests ornamenting several doorways that led to the gathering rooms where Jacob entertained his guests. The Whooley crest was a gauntlet with a falcon, set upon a wreath with twists of silver and green resting on top of a knight's steel helmet. The motto, *Manus Haec Inimica Tyrannis*, loosely translated as: "This hand shall only be raised in anger against a tyrant or tyranny itself."

Jacob took enormous pride in his ancestry. Greylocke Castle in Yorkshire had been home to the Whooley family for twelve generations, and the bloodline could be traced all the way back to William the Conqueror. He revered the old ways and dreamed of a return to that era, but that was impossible. Instead he surrounded himself with a house and grounds that were reminders of more noble times, which included a spectacular wine cellar that his father had excavated in a natural cavern upon which the manor house rested.

The wine cellar was a seldom-viewed manifestation of Jacob's other self-indulgence: he was a connoisseur when it came to selecting wines from the best vineyards of Europe. Before the troubles with England, he had acquired vast selections from Germany, Italy, Portugal, and Spain, but it was the French wines for which he had the highest regard. Wines from the several different regions in France were meant to accompany food and complemented his gourmet appetite. On this night, however, he would serve a simple baguette with locally produced cheese to prepare the palate.

A loud knock at the front entrance announced the guests' arrival. Whooley opened the door. "Mr. Preble, please come in with your distinguished friend."

Gallimet followed Preble into the foyer, removed his hat, and bowed. "It is my privilege, monsieur." As he spoke he glanced appreciatively around the room at the pageantry of its decor and regally appointed furnishings. "I have looked forward to this moment since receiving your kind invitation."

"The pleasure is mine, Mr. Gallimet. I have heard much about your talent since your arrival in Haverhill. But please come into my library, where the fire is warm and I can offer you a small collation."

Inside the library, medieval suits of armor guarded opposite corners, and banners displaying the coats of arms of Knights Templar hung from the walls in between shelves that held volumes of leather-bound books. On an English sideboard rested a silver tray with the baguette and cheese wheel. To the right a pewter wine dish held an open bottle of Bordeaux accompanied by two long-stem goblets made of cut glass. Whooley presented Preble with a tankard of ale before carefully filling approximately two-thirds of each goblet with the medium, almost brick-red burgundy, one for his guest and the other for himself.

"To your good health, sir," Whooley toasted.

Gallimet took a sip and stirred the liquid in his mouth for an instant before swallowing.

"*Magnifique*," he announced under his breath.

"We live in troublesome times, Gallimet. These writs imposed by England mean that superb wines like these have become scarce. Meanwhile, our patriot friends dump tea in the harbor, which only serves to infuriate the English toward more restrictive measures."

"A terrible sacrifice, monsieur," Gallimet nodded.

"A sacrifice indeed—these are the very symbols and privileges that connect men of standing to their mother country, links that my family never anticipated would be broken when they came to the New World and were accorded this family seat. Some Americans have had a change of heart and mind when it comes to England. They want to free themselves of the ties that bind us and declare a new civilization of free and able men. Well, good enough, but wines define civilization, Gallimet; they express a certain enlightenment." Whooley motioned for the Frenchman to come closer, then relaxed his voice. "Would you care to see for yourself, Mr. Gallimet?"

"Oui, monsieur," Gallimet whispered. Whooley turned to the bookshelves and pulled at a red leather-bound volume. Suddenly the shelf and wainscoting pivoted, revealing a dark, narrow entrance.

"Join me now, gentlemen." Gallimet and Preble followed as they descended a wooden staircase that went down four risers to a small landing, then down again for eight more. At the bottom Whooley lit first one lamp, then three more. One was portable; he carried it into an enormous catacomb where one wine rack after another stood, some holding as many as twelve bottles across and ten high. Gallimet observed that they were arranged by region: one rack devoted to wines of Portugal, another Spain, and yet another Italy. But the largest stock were the rows of French wines.

Gallimet was mesmerized by the extent of the collection as he gradually became aware of the cavity in which he stood. The walls were damp and covered with saltpeter, just like the caves at the mines. He wondered if they were related. In England some natural caverns like these were rumored to be ley tunnels, subterranean passages that ran under major obstacles like rivers and lakes. Legends about their existence usually involved improbable passages that connected country houses, castles, churches, and other medieval buildings, along with esoteric notions that they were channels or paths of the earth's energy.

"Savor the plum, Gallimet," Jacob declared loudly as he filled two more goblets, "and tell me about your life and remarkable journey to America."

The Frenchman sat on the bench, stretched out his legs, and gazed at the treasure of wines that surrounded him. He sipped, then reminisced about his youth in France, offered his opinion of the new king, Louis XVI, and told of his migration to America with French Huguenots. Whooley was equal to the conversation, and an hour passed easily while the wine flowed. With little prodding, Gallimet began to boast of the talents that had brought him to Haverhill. Jacob refilled his goblet and remarked in a disarming tone, "You strike me, sir, an educated man."

"*Oui*, monsieur, I studied at the Academy of Sciences in Paris, before departing to fulfill family obligations."

"So you're a scientist and an artist."

"An artist by day and a chemist by night," Gallimet said with a slight slur of inebriation.

"In the West Parish?" Jacob led him.

"Ah, you know about the mines, then."

"Just that there was some kind of setback." Whooley was fishing, and his guest took the bait.

"No setback, monsieur, just a small explosion," Gallimet retorted. "I have the process perfected; my powder is superior." His eyelids were heavy now, his speech labored. Jacob had the confirmation he needed and glanced at Preble, who took the cue.

"All right, Frenchie, it's time for you and me to take leave of our fine host. It's getting late and it will be a hard pull if the river ebbs and the tide turns on me ferry. And take your shoes off so we don't track no dirt through Mr. Whooley's nice house."

Bart Preble had led a storied life—too storied to separate fact from fiction. He declared himself, on several occasions, to be the son of Anne Bonny, the famous pirate who had sailed the Caribbean with the legendary Calico Jack Rackham. Bonny had reportedly given birth to a bastard son in Cuba, but Bart had no evidence to support his claim that he was that child. He grew up in South Carolina and, at fifteen, hired on to a schooner out of Charleston bound for the West Indies. By his account, the ship was struck by a whale on the return voyage and sank so quickly that he and six other crewmen had no time to take on provisions or water. They drifted for six days in the tropical sun, and three crewmen died of thirst before making land. Only Bart and two other crewmen survived the ordeal. He later wandered up and down Appalachia and claimed to have served under Francis Marion, the "Swamp Fox," in a campaign against the Cherokee. He arrived in Haverhill around 1762, but until he met Jacob Whooley, his barge on the Merrimack was the closest he came to any sort of adventure like those he boasted of in the southern colonies.

When Jacob needed an intermediary to represent him in his business affairs with smugglers, Bart Preble was a perfect agent to do his bidding. Acquiring a few bottles of imported wine from Benjamin Davis was one thing, but the provisioners who could adequately stock Whooley's inventory were often thieves or pirates, not the sort of businessmen with whom he could be seen dealing. Bart, on the other hand, had the untidy means of contact and the guile required to complete the transaction and deliver the goods to the manor house without attracting attention. Everything went smoothly until the British occupation of Boston began making procurement difficult, driving up the cost, and making such extravagance more than even Jacob could afford.

During a visit with a Newburyport lawyer, Jacob learned that a young British officer was paying informants to reveal the clandestine movements of contraband, including small caches of munitions, along the seaside towns of Cape Ann. Not only that, but Jacob learned that these informants were often the same smugglers who were plying him with exorbitantly priced goods to fill his wine cellar. This gave him an idea: why not furnish consistent and reliable information to this ambitious British officer in direct exchange for goods that would otherwise circumvent customs, and thereby cut out the middleman, restore the Crown's stream of tax collections, and provide Whooley Manor with a sustainable source of excellent wines?

The plan dictated, however, that Bart's new role be marginal. A business exchange with smugglers was one thing; a negotiation with a representative of King George was quite another matter. In this arrangement Bart would be the messenger— the appointments secretary, so to speak—and Jacob would have to orchestrate the arrangement personally, but how? People would view any association that Jacob had with the British as an act of treachery, even though his intentions were benign. Jacob thought about this and decided that he would need a hidden identity, a persona behind a name: the Kestrel.

Although this meant Bart's remuneration would be less rewarding, he was still the purveyor of gossip and information. The added opportunity for mischief this new situation presented was not lost on wily Bart Preble.

General Gage was staring at a map of the Massachusetts Bay Colony and the area of the Merrimack Valley in particular. He was anxious for news about the powder source from Hannibal Jones's informant. Defiance was spreading among the so-called Sons of Liberty even before the Continental Congress convened in Philadelphia. Agitators were in hiding somewhere outside of Boston, treasonous men who disparaged the apparatus and symbols of British authority. They were, he had no doubt, building an arsenal to arm the Americans in the event of rebellion.

At just this moment, Lieutenant Jones appeared at the doorway of Gage's headquarters.

"Ah, come in, come in, Lieutenant. I am about to serve tea; please join me."

"Thank you, sir."

Gage sat and gestured for Jones to do the same. "What news do you bring from our spy?"

"I found a sealed letter in my quarters this morning, delivered surreptitiously while I made my regimental inspection. It is from the Kestrel." Gage arched his brow in a way that Jones interpreted as permission to continue speaking. "The Kestrel says there is a chemist, an expert in powdermaking, who was brought in from France to oversee production of a vast mining operation located somewhere in the valley: three hundred barrels per month. The stores are being shipped downriver to Newburyport and offloaded to several other vessels from there." Gage was growing impatient.

"But where is the source, Lieutenant? I do not mean to have the Royal Navy chasing down every ship or barge from Cape Ann to Plymouth Harbor."

"He guards his hand closely and lays down his chips judiciously, sir. I suspect he is withholding some information to remain valuable to us."

"Well, threaten him with a flogging, Lieutenant," Gage responded petulantly.

"I do not believe that will work with this man, General. However, I suspect he has an accomplice; someone was seen entering my quarters as an inconspicuous tradesman who could have delivered the Kestrel's letter. My informants are investigating as we speak."

October arrived and Dolly was perturbed. It had been weeks since she had engaged her spy, and she had not seen or heard from him since his appearance at the meetinghouse. She was not about to be ignored, and so she changed and headed down the hill to the wharves. On this excursion a half moon illuminated the night sky as she made her way across the pier to the place where Bart Preble kept his ferry. The ferry and barge were tied up at the usual spot, but there was no sign of Preble. The nearby shack that Bart kept as a warming hut and shelter was darkened, but she thought to look inside in case he was sleeping off an evening of socialization at the tavern. It was vacant.

Retracing her steps, she skipped across the wharf, when something caught her eye. Between the two adjacent wharves was a gap of about two and a half feet, enough room so that the two would not rub up against each other in a gale but close enough for a small catwalk to allow access from one to the other without someone's having to go all the way up one gangway and down the other. Something was stuck in between, and the current caused just enough drag against the catwalk to force it to an odd angle, making passage difficult. It looked like a large peddler's pack, and if Dolly were going to get across to the long wharf, she would have to dislodge it.

A boat hook at the back of the wharf was handy, so she grabbed it and guided it underneath the catwalk and pushed against the obstruction. It wouldn't budge. She maneuvered to the other side and worked the boat hook around the object until it fastened itself to some extremity. She pulled hard three or four times until it finally came loose and slowly rolled over like a giant cork. Dolly leaned in to examine the goods, then let out a shriek as Bart Preble stared up at her, his lifeless eyes protruding from a bloated, vacant face.

Sam was summoned to the wharf, where a small group of men were gathered around the body. He lifted a canvas tarpaulin and examined the corpse. There were no obvious signs of a struggle, but it was too dark to tell. Henry Morse, the town physician, would perform a physical examination in the morning and report his findings to Sam and Colonel Rollins. Sam spied Dolly seated near the gangway above, and he walked up to the pier and extended both hands.

"Are you all right?"

"Yes, I'm fine, Sam, just a bit shaken." Sam sat down next to her on a makeshift bench.

"I need to ask a few questions. Are you willing or would you rather that I wait until the morning?"

Dolly shook her head. "I'm fine. What do you want to know?"

"Well, first of all, tell me what you were doing down here at night."

"The night air was brisk and the moon half full, so I decided to walk down to the river, as I sometimes do. When I reached the pier I noticed something in the water and decided to investigate. Turns out it was poor Bart Preble."

"The wharves seem like an unusual place for the parson's wife to be on most nights, Mrs. Makepeace."

"You may call me Dolly, Sam, and I think you know me well enough to know that I am not in fear of the myths and rumors that circulate throughout this town about the wharves."

Sam pushed the interrogation further. "Bart was a wharf rat, so you must have encountered him on your other visits."

Dolly eyed Sam as if to concede a secret. "Mr. Preble could separate the wheat from the chaff when it came to the gossip of the village, Sam. I paid him generously on more than one occasion to shed light on matters that were of consequence to me."

"And did he always fulfill his obligation to you?"

Dolly looked at him and let out a sigh. "Obviously not this time."

"What was the mission that you sent him on this time?"

Dolly's head ached as she placed her forehead in her right hand and rubbed before responding. "I hired him to find out what was going on in the West Parish. I feared that Asa had involved himself in some sort of counterintelligence that he would regret. And after your visit I suspected that it had to do with some covert activity in the West Parish."

"What made you think that Parson Pike might be involved in espionage?"

"Not as a spy—he would never consciously betray his neighbors. But religion and politics are sometimes strange bedfellows. Baptists and other reformists have created disorder and discord that have startled the Anglicans. He believes that it is his calling to broker peace, and I worry that could lead to an unwitting involvement in whatever intrigue is evolving out on the frontier."

"Anything else?"

"Yes. He seemed particularly anxious about Paul Gallimet. I don't know the reason why, but I told this to Bart Preble and suggested that he investigate his background."

"Where is your husband now, Dolly?"

"I cannot say, exactly. He has taken to traveling from one parish to the next to counteract what he considers itinerant forces that are stirring up trouble, but he always makes sure that he is back for Sunday services and prayer."

Sinkholes

Dee was studying a file that she had retrieved online from the Haverhill Public Library. The HPL Special Collections were renowned in Essex County as a treasure trove of historic information, archived and indexed over several decades. More recently, a system of digital data storage had made it possible to research everything from genealogy to local architecture online. If it had historical value, it was most likely in the database; you just had to know how to drill down and find it. Dee was a writer, adept at researching her subject matter, whether that meant online, in the stacks of a college library, or out knocking on doors, and her fascination with her ancestor was obsessive, with the diary continually revealing clues to a saga she could hardly ignore. She emailed Arthur periodically, keeping him abreast of her findings, a friendly correspondent to encourage her in her efforts. He had made a gift of the diary before Dee left for home, for which she was now deeply indebted.

"Aunt Dolly's diary speaks of considerable drama down on the wharves, even a dead body. It seems there was much cloak-and-dagger activity." Dee had taken to calling her protagonist Aunt Dolly or Auntie, as a way of keeping her close yet apart from her own identity. "There was some kind of a skirmish near Haverhill, and Sam Dearborn was right in the thick of it, according to one entry. It looks as though some kind of defensive action was taken to protect stores of gunpowder."

Later she wrote: "This gunpowder thing is perplexing. From one report that I found in the state archives, it sounds like there was a substantial mining operation somewhere near the Little River, but I can't find any other historical information to support it."

Arthur's curiosity was aroused, so he borrowed an old map of Haverhill from the library. The Little River was clearly marked, but above it and just west something was written in letters too small to read. He grabbed a magnifying glass from his desk, and the word became barely legible: "sinkholes." He called Dee that evening to report his discovery.

"They would appear to be on Long Hill, although I've never heard mention of any such topography in that part of town."

"Well, Auntie mentions suspicious activity in the West Parish in her diary, and this sounds suspiciously westward."

"Perhaps a little firsthand exploration might be worth the journey," Arthur ventured. The glow from Dee's childhood was once again stirring.

"If you will take me in, Uncle Arthur, I think I'll plan another family visit to the old town."

∙ ∙ ∙

October 5, 1774 — Rain clouds and a damp chill have settled in. A terrible fate has befallen Mr. Preble, and I fear that I have somehow set in motion forces that threaten the very foundation of our town. Colonel Rollins and Captain Dearborn are good men whom we trust and admire to lead us in the face of adversity, yet I pray for God's guidance. No word from Asa.

The next day Sam would meet with Colonel Rollins to describe the events of the previous evening, including his conversation with Dolly. He was trying to add it all up. Bart Preble was a vagrant and idle as often as he was working the ferry. He was undependable, yet not without some measure of guile. Sam considered that he might have fallen off the wharf and drowned after a night out at the Freemason's Arm, but no one there remembered seeing him. If it was not an accident, what motive could there be for his murder? It was certainly not robbery.

Sam decided to search the shed near the ferry where Bart usually slept. It was not much more than a warming hut, a shack at the bottom of Kent Street with a stove, a broken chair, and two casks that served as tabletops. A mariner's hammock was stretched across the room just above an old half barrel that was the largest piece of furniture in the place. Sam looked inside and found blankets, assorted articles of clothing, and a pair of boots. Further down was a pack that contained a pot, several tin cups, assorted knives, combs, and thread spools. In the middle of this accumulation, his hand grasped a bottle, which he removed from the bundle. It was a Bandol rosé from Provence, still corked.

Sam was no connoisseur, but he knew that French wines were not likely to be among Bart's usual drinking habits. Something else caught his attention as well: in the sunlight shining through the open door, he could see fresh soot on the leather soles of the boots. Heavy soot deposits were present at the saltpeter mines and most underground caves. He tucked the bottle into the boots and started up the hill.

When he reached the common, Sam encountered Ben Davis, the merchant who had helped with the plan at the loading docks. Davis was no stranger to deception, as he regularly smuggled goods like molasses, tea, and coffee to avoid the prohibitive taxes that England imposed. On this day he was seething.

"Yesterday custom officials stopped a schooner that arrived in Newburyport from the West Indies with a large quantity of molasses, sugarcane, and rum. The cargo, much of which was destined for my mercantile, was confiscated. Someone had to have alerted the British, Sam."

"What was the reaction in Newburyport?" Sam asked.

"Outrage. A crowd gathered and several custom officials were roughed up. The Tories are demanding that Gage send troops as protection, but I see it as an excuse to disrupt our trading operations."

And our powder smuggling, Sam thought. "Who else knew about the schooner and its cargo?"

"Well, Bart Preble, for one; I often hire him to offload goods from the wharf to my storage cellar. I think we had better have a conversation with the scoundrel and prepare the tar and feathers."

"Bart's dead. We found his body in the river between the wharves last night."

"Well, that's an interesting coincidence. What was the cause of his demise?"

"I don't know. Henry Morse examined the corpse this morning and should be reporting his findings to Colonel Rollins. I'm on my way there now. Why don't you join me?"

Thomas Rollins's home was a short distance north of the village, and the two men walked the route easily in about ten minutes. The house was a garrison that Thomas's father had built during the Indian uprisings. A chimney was located at each end of the house, which had three rooms upstairs and three rooms down. The woodwork was elaborate; the home's richness reflected prominence.

Rollins greeted them at the entryway. "Good morning, Sam. I see you have brought along my friend Mr. Davis."

"It's anything but a good morning, Thomas," Davis sputtered. "I have distressing news from Newburyport." He repeated what he had told Dearborn about the schooner and the confiscation of goods on the previous day.

"This on top of Bart Preble's dead body makes for an interesting day," Sam observed drily. Rollins mulled over the news.

"I doubt that General Gage will reassign any troops to Newburyport," Rollins said. "He has his hands full in Boston. I will see if we can find out what has prompted this activity. If they were really looking for our goods, then we have been doubly betrayed. As for the ferryman's demise, Henry Morse is prepared to give us a report. He's in the next room."

"Single shot with a flintlock pistol at fairly close range," Morse stated matter-of-factly. "I found no water in his lungs, so he probably died instantly and his body was dumped into the river."

"Why do you say that? Maybe he fell into the river where he was shot," Sam remarked.

"Well, that's what puzzles me: he was barefoot and there were fresh abrasions on the heels of his feet, like he'd been dragged some distance."

Rollins could see that Sam's interest was stirred; he said nothing of it but concluded that Sam was on to something. "Thank you, gentlemen. Ben, I will keep you informed if I learn more about the seizure. Meanwhile, why don't you hitch a ride with Henry; I'd like for Sam to remain here to brief me on several other matters."

When the visitors departed, Colonel Rollins invited Sam to the kitchen, where he had prepared a pot of tea.

"What's your theory on all of this, Sam?"

"No theories, Colonel, just intuition. I searched Bart's shed for clues this morning. I found these." Sam held up the boots with the wine tucked neatly inside one of them. Rollins removed the bottle.

"Bandol rosé—somewhat extravagant for Bart's tastes."

"And it is unopened, as though he was saving it for some other purpose than to satisfy his own thirst."

"A gift?" Rollins wondered aloud.

"I've never known Bart to be especially generous. More likely a quid pro quo," Sam replied.

"Yes, but with whom?" Rollins poured hot tea into two china cups with saucers and sat down at the table. He placed one before his guest. "And those are the boots that he was not wearing when his body was pulled from the river?"

"So it would seem. What is more interesting is what is on the shoe leather." Sam turned the boots over to reveal fresh soot on the sole of each. "This soot is nasty stuff. I have to clean it off my own boots every time I visit the mines, or I end up tracking it through the household."

"So you believe that Mr. Preble may have been sneaking around our operations?"

"I can't think of any other explanation," Sam acknowledged.

Rollins stared down at his cup and stirred slowly, as if reading the tealeaves. "I think it's time for a plan that will smoke out any infiltrators."

When Sam left Colonel Rollins and returned to the village, he stopped in at Harrod's and the Freemason's Arm. The tavern was as good a place as any to try to piece together Bart Preble's movements.

Mrs. Hartshorne was sweeping the floors as Sam entered. "Good morning, Lizzie," he said.

"Morning to you, Sam. What brings you here this time of day, as if I couldn't guess?"

"You heard about Bart?"

"It's the talk of the village. A terrible thing, even for the likes of Mr. Preble. How could a ferryman fall in and drown like that?"

Sam said nothing in response—no sense in creating a panic over murder and mayhem so close to Harrod's. "Can you recall the last time Bart was here?"

"Sure I do. It was Thursday night, but he didn't stay long. Had a tankard, maybe two, with that artist Gallimet, then left soon afterwards."

Sam considered this odd. Preble and Gallimet had little in common. The thought that Bart might have been following Dolly's lead crossed his mind, but a direct confrontation seemed out of character for Bart. He liked to stalk his prey and learn of their activities by more covert means.

"What was the Frenchman drinking?"

"Madeira, same as always. He complains about the wine, but he's not one for ale."

"Did he stay late?"

"No, just long enough to have some supper before retiring. He seemed in good spirits."

Sam thanked her before leaving. "By the way, do you store any French wines?"

"Not a drop. Ben Davis might smuggle a few bottles now and then, but I think he sells most of those to Jacob Whooley."

Sam stabled his horse at Harrod's, so he was able to head for the West Parish and the sinkholes without delay, as he and Colonel Rollins had planned. When he arrived, Ephraim and the Frenchman were busy overseeing the mixing, measuring, and pouring of nitrates into several casks.

"Captain Dearborn, what brings you here today?" Ephraim asked, hardly looking up.

"I'm here to take inventory. We're planning another excursion downriver and we will need a full boatload. Two brigantines are meeting us for the transfer."

"That's a big undertaking; where are they bound?" Ephraim asked.

"Providence and New London. We're extending our distribution farther south." This was a fabrication, but Rollins and Dearborn knew it would draw a response should the word reach General Gage. The cargo would be switched at the last moment, and if the British boarded the old sloop in Newburyport they would find nothing more than a few dozen barrels of molasses and Rollins would know there was a leak. If there was no interdiction, they would assume that their cover was intact.

"I suppose you heard the news about Bart Preble," Sam added. Ephraim shook his head with a puzzled expression. "He turned up dead down by the wharves, cause not known."

Now Gallimet reacted. He pushed his spectacles up to his forehead and stared straight ahead before resuming his work. Finally he spoke.

"I saw Mr. Preble the other night, Captain. He seemed a perfectly healthy man, so I hope it was not the result of some misfortune."

"An investigation is being undertaken to determine the means of death. We won't know anything more until it is complete. May I ask what business you had with Preble?"

"He provided me with a crossing on the ferry, nothing more."

Just then, several of the teamsters arrived to begin loading casks that would make their way to the sloop *Naomi* for the pretentious journey. It was bad timing. Sam hoped to learn more from Gallimet, who was obviously troubled by the news of Bart's fate, but the interruption apparently caused the Frenchman to believe he had said too much already. He offered no further explanation, other than something about a portrait session with Jacob Whooley.

Most churches in New England eschewed extreme emotionalism, but recently there had been a schism in Asa Pike's congregation. Some parishioners, favoring fire and brimstone, were defecting in small but troubling numbers to the Baptists. To add insult to injury, some of these detractors supported the notion of revolution, since they hoped the cause would bring religious as well as political freedom.

Earlier in the day Asa had confronted Daniel Swan of East Bradford, who had proclaimed himself a lay preacher outside any established order, as far as Asa could determine. It had been an unpleasant conversation, and he thought himself fortunate to have escaped without harm. Now, as he neared the cow common on the south side of the Merrimack, the clamoring of hooves startled him. Six men on horseback traveled the Post Road at a distinctly military gait, wearing the red tunics and leather-crested helmets of the King's light cavalry. They were followed by a war wagon drawn by two draft horses hauling a cargo that was covered by canvas. Baptists and now Redcoats—the day couldn't get any worse, Asa thought to himself. In spite of his annoyance, he decided he should investigate and he tied the mare to the fence, proceeding ahead on foot.

Asa wandered a few rods off the road, just inside the orchard to the south of Jacob Whooley's manor house. After trudging about a quarter mile he could see the steeds, still saddled, grazing in the pound behind the stable, and out of the sight of anyone who might be looking across the river from the village.

The wagon's cargo had been removed, and a number of sturdy wooden boxes were stacked neatly near the residence. Asa moved in for a closer inspection. Prying open one of the boxes, he found several bottles packed and cushioned with straw. Carefully removing one, he rotated it to read the label: Château Margaux, a claret from one of the finest vineyards in France. Why, he wondered, was the British cavalry escorting stores of French wine to Whooley Manor?

Since the riders were nowhere to be seen, he crept up to have a look through the back window. Inside, five of the Redcoats were seated around a table in the kitchen, consuming loaves of bread, pulled pork, and tankards of ale. He did not see Jacob and imagined that he might be in some sort of predicament, so he slipped around the corner of the house to where he knew Whooley kept his study. Shinnying up an old oak tree, he spied Jacob sharing a glass of wine with a young officer, the apparent leader of the company, and another soldier. He could not hear voices, but it appeared to be a cordial conversation with smiles and even a toast of some sort. If he could manage to get closer to the window, he thought, he might be able to overhear the men.

Carefully he angled his way to the house, but the window was too high. He looked around and found a bucket, inverted it, and stepped up carefully, placing his ear close to the windowpane.

"There is much more where this came from, as long as your information remains accurate and improves its value, Goodman Whooley."

"Have I disappointed you thus far, Lieutenant Jones?"

"No, but you have been unable or perhaps unwilling to disclose the source of the gunpowder. Until we know the location of the manufactory, this will be a never-ending game of cat and mouse."

"When I learn of the location I will reveal it, Lieutenant. But I must have some assurances as to what the consequences would be to those who are found responsible for this smuggling operation."

"I have no say in that, sir."

"As was the fate you dealt Mr. Preble?"

"He was an impostor and an extortionist. He got what he deserved, and you should be thankful. If General Gage had gotten to him first, you would have been exposed in a moment's notice."

Asa was dumbfounded. That Jacob Whooley could betray his neighbors was unthinkable. Could he have heard wrong? He pressed forward to hear more, when suddenly the bottom of the bucket gave way, sending him to the ground with an audible *crash*. Jones dashed to the window, then called out to his men. In an instant Parson Pike became a captive, and no slight liability to Whooley and whatever arrangements he had with the British Army.

October 11, 1774 — Partly sunny and windy. Asa has been gone for five days now and I am worried. Sam Dearborn is busy with his farm and his command, but he has always regarded my requests with satisfaction. If I ask for his aid, I feel certain he will endeavor to find my husband.

Asa had been missing since just before Bart Preble's mysterious demise, and Dolly had no word of his whereabouts. Usually someone with whom he had crossed paths would stop by to say they had seen Parson Pike in such and such a parish and yes, he was making his way home. This time there had been no such communication, and the events at the wharf had Dolly concerned. Sam Dearborn was on horseback near the parsonage, when she waved him over. He pulled up and guided the sorrel to the corner of the porch, where she stood with her arms folded.

"Sorry to bother you, Sam, but Asa is long overdue from his mission and I'm worried."

"What was his itinerary?"

"East Parish to Cottle's Ferry, then Bradford and home again."

"Who was he looking for in Bradford?"

"Daniel Swan, among others. He's proclaimed himself lay preacher, and Asa meant to have a talk with him about it."

Sam was wary. The Swan men were ruffians and troublemakers. They burned down fences they didn't like and moved stone boundaries they didn't agree with.

"I have to pilot the sloop downriver today, but if he does not return by nightfall I'll cross over to Bradford in the morning and see what I can find out."

"Thank you, Sam."

Sam stabled his horse at Harrod's, then walked to the riverfront, where the sloop *Naomi* was being readied for its illusory voyage. It was a gambit to see if espionage was at play, but an essential one in Sam's mind. As he approached the wharf he saw Ben Davis overseeing the loading process. Davis was irritated since he and several other merchant's had to underwrite the demurrage or risk increased assessments and he grumbled a curt greeting.

Sam boarded the vessel and a glint of light flashed across his line of sight, a reflection emanating from somewhere up high on the Bradford side of the Merrimack. He wondered if it was a signal and, if so, to whom and for what purpose.

Just then, the boatswain's pipe sounded to clear the decks. "We are full to the gunwales and ready to cast off, Mr. Davis," the boatswain's mate shouted. "Any words of wisdom for our friends at the Custom House?"

"Tell them to keep their bloody hands off my goods or they'll have a real rebellion to contend with." Davis shook his fist in the air, causing Sam to laugh out loud for the first time in days.

Husbandmen largely populated Newbury, but since those who lived near the water were mostly merchants and traders, the general court had granted them separation and Newburyport was established as a separate town. With three shipyards and a numerous ferries, the harbor here was busy. Ships arrived from all over the Atlantic seaboard, all the way to the West Indies and back, importing molasses and exporting the rum produced from it in the local distilleries. If the transfer from the *Naomi* went routinely, half the cargo of molasses would be loaded onto one of two brigantines that sat silently in the harbor. That load would later be delivered to friendly merchants in Boston, while the rest would remain onboard as ballast to be returned to Ben Davis as planned.

Sam breathed a sigh of relief when the last cask was offloaded. It had been a long day, and he felt good that the voyage had gone without incident. On the way back, he relaxed and enjoyed the scenery as the sloop sailed swiftly homeward with a steady breeze and favorable tide. The river had always provided some of life's pleasantest sensations. He could lean back and listen to the current lapping against the boat's planking while staring at the clouds and studying each formation, sometimes imagining a bird or a whale or some mythical creature. Every bend promised new discoveries, with low-lying islands providing habitat for rough-legged hawks, northern shrike, and an occasional snowy owl.

This is a wonderfully rich land, he thought. He would have to settle down and pay more attention to cultivating the soil once the troubles with England were over. He would find a wife and raise a family on the property he had inherited in the East Parish.

They were less than a mile distant, and Sam could see the farmhouse when something below shifted and interrupted his stream of consciousness. As he lowered himself into the cargo hold to investigate, several barrels came unlashed without warning and knocked him backward, pinning him to the dingy wet planking. The boatswain's mate reacted quickly and called to a crewman, but the barrels were awkward and it took several minutes to free him from the sheer weight of the molasses. The crew dragged him to the forecastle and laid him out on the bunk. Sam's head was pounding and he could hear nothing, except for a loud pitch that screamed from one ear to the other. The turmoil around him was a blur, and then there was nothing, just darkness and the sensation that he was adrift.

The mare and carriage were retrieved and placed in the stable before Hannibal Jones and his company started back to Boston. Asa was under house arrest, for all intents and purposes, and kept under lock and key in the tack room next to the horse stalls. His capture and interrogation had been swift, and the British officer had questioned him closely about stores of gunpowder, any knowledge of which he had adamantly disavowed. He could not help but think of the infamous Gunpowder Plot of 1605, when Guy Fawkes was imprisoned in the Tower of London and tortured into confession for guarding thirty-six barrels of gunpowder meant to assassinate King James I. Asa had heard his father commemorate the sordid event many times in sermons, and now he imagined himself at similar risk of being hanged, drawn, and quartered.

But as the days passed, so did his angst. There was no sign of Hannibal Jones, and Jacob was a benevolent, if not downright kind, gaoler. Likewise, Asa proved to be a model prisoner.

In the weeks that followed, Jacob found that he enjoyed Asa's company immensely. He shared his books and almanacs and they discussed the great writers, as well as the politics of the day. They played chess late into the afternoons, before enjoying one of the wines Jacob selected to complement their evening dinner. Asa, likewise, found his host to be a stimulating conversationalist and discovered they had more common ground in their opinions than not. Eventually he gave Jacob his word that he would attempt no escape, in exchange for the freedom to move about the house and the sleeping quarters on the second floor.

Asa found much time for contemplation, and so he thought about his boyhood in Ipswich. He had lived on a long straight road that led directly to the meetinghouse where his father preached on Sundays. Along the way there was a bend in the highway that he had never pursued, where lay a path that was lined with wild roses and beach plums. He wondered about that crooked lane so often that one day it got the best of him. He followed the trail for a good distance until it ended, then wandered barefoot through the sand dunes and grass until he found a steady breeze, smelled the salty air, and heard the roar of the ocean, but he went no further. It was forbidden.

I should return to Ipswich next summer, he thought while reposing in Jacob's hospitable captivity. *I can find that path and smell the salty air, hear the roar and see the ocean. I will take my shoes off and walk through the tidal flow and lie down on the sandbars and let the waves soak me.*

In spite of their newfound friendship, Asa was troubled by Jacob's activities and decided to confront him on the subject. A glass of port segued into the subject of honor, fidelity, and loyalty to one's neighbor.

"You know, Jacob, the fires that burn within these patriots have not caused me to bear any ill will whatsoever toward England. However, when a fellow citizen chooses a different road than the one we travel, it cannot be cause for treason at the expense of the lives and fortunes of our friends and neighbors."

"Is that what you think, Asa? That I am a loyalist, a Tory with no conscience?"

"Why else would you consort with the likes of Hannibal Jones—a deal with the devil?"

"Balderdash! I give Jones minor information: a schooner with stolen rum and molasses destined for Ben Davis's cellar; information on ammunition supply lines that they already suspect and I simply confirm. I am no traitor, Parson Pike; I simply take information that is a day old and a dollar short and deal it for the right to pursue a civilized existence."

"And what about Bart Preble, Jacob—didn't he deserve the right to his pursuits?"

Whooley was silent for a moment, then pursed his lips before responding. "Bart was my confidential source. I paid him generously to help me confirm and convey information that would suit my purposes. But he became greedy and tried to perpetrate a scheme on his own. He took my nom de guerre to extort money from the British. Lieutenant Jones was onto him quickly and set a trap. He killed him right there with a single shot from that flintlock pistol that I keep on the mantel, then dragged his body down to the ferry and dumped him on the Haverhill side to divert attention. Unfortunately, Bart had his boots off, as he always did when he visited the cellar. Jones overlooked them, so I took them across early the next morning, the long way, and deposited them into a barrel in his shack. So I guess I am complicit in that part."

"But how did Jones know of the deception? And how did he find you?" Asa asked.

"Because I used the name Kestrel, he knew it was I and that Bart had to be an impostor. Do you see that crest carved above the doorway? A gauntlet with a falcon, set upon a wreath resting on top of a knight's steel helmet. Well, any Whooley worth his salt knows it's not just a damn falcon, it's a kestrel, and Lieutenant Hannibal Whooley Jones had me figured out right from the start."

When the alarm spread that there had been an accident onboard the *Naomi* and that Sam was injured, Dolly rushed down to the wharf.

Henry Morse had arrived minutes earlier and was stanching the blood from Sam's nose when she arrived. "A broken nose is the least of it, Dolly. He's unconscious, and I'm afraid there may be internal injuries to his skull. We need to get these wounds dressed and place his head in a slightly upright resting position to keep the blood from gathering in the brain."

"Bring him to the parsonage, Henry; we have a clean guest room where I can look after him."

An oxcart served as ambulance to transport Sam up the hill with Dolly at his side. Henry stopped at his apothecary for ointments and herbal remedies that would treat the external wounds. When he arrived at the parsonage, he began removing the patient's clothes, causing Dolly to blush and avert her eyes.

"No time for modesty now, Dolly," Henry barked. "We've got a badly injured man here who needs our attention. I can see some bruising around his ribcage, so I need your help wrapping it as a precaution."

By the time they were done, two pillows propped up Sam's bandaged head and he was taking in and expelling slow, uneven breaths. Dolly closed the shutters partially in order to restrain the late-afternoon sunlight that filled the room.

"He needs rest now. Check on him every hour or so to see if his breathing settles. If he starts to fever, wet towels around the head and neck should help."

"Henry," Dolly asked, "what do you think are his chances?"

"Depends on how long before he comes to. The later he's like this, the worse. I found blood coming from his ears, and if it's a swelling in the cranium that's causing this, I'm going to have to relieve it somehow." That would be a risky course, and Dolly knew it. Trepanation was a common procedure in which a small hole was drilled into the skull to reduce pressure, but any mistake could leave the patient dimwitted or worse.

For two days and two more nights, she nursed her patient with Henry Morse looking in daily. Sam's mind wandered in and out of consciousness, and night sweats and pain disturbed his sleep. When he did sleep he dreamed about his boyhood on the farm and of his father, the most capable man he had ever known. When it came to riding, hunting, and predicting weather, there was no man his match. He had taught Sam and his brother to fish for sturgeon on the banks of the big river and how to build a campfire using just enough wood to stay warm yet not enough to reveal a presence, lest any hostile observers might happen by. Yes, Joshua Dearborn was the quintessential American, skilled and industrious, devoted to family, faith, and community.

He left home in the spring of 1757 to command a Massachusetts company sent to relieve British forces at Fort William Henry. By August the French forces of General Montcalm had laid siege to the garrison and the British and Americans were forced to surrender. In a notorious act of treachery, French Indian allies violated the terms of an agreement and massacred a column of unarmed men as they left the fort.

Sam was just ten at the time, and his father's death came as a devastating blow. It was a watershed event that would define his character for the rest of his life. He ran away from home for five days and lived in a lean-to at the upper end of the Little River. There, he caught eels and ate them raw, like the Indians his father had told stories about when they explored the sinkholes. Inside the caves were bats, thousands of them. Sam watched them fly about at dusk, darting above in a chaos that seemed to reflect his life. He had to seek order by escaping the chaos, he thought to himself. It was the moral way of a free society—it was what his father would have expected of him.

From that moment on, Sam pledged a certain duty not only to his family, but also to his neighbors and fellow townsmen, to repel any danger and oppose any foe that might threaten the prosperous and orderly survival of their settlement, especially outsiders whom he distrusted.

A harsh autumn wind rattled the sash, and Sam awakened to see Dolly at the window with a full moon silhouetting her girlish figure through a gauzy nightgown. He looked, sighed, and then slept some more.

The blood seeping from his ears stopped, as did the night sweats. Finally, on Monday morning, Dolly was dozing in the rocker at his bedside when she heard something.

"How long have I been inconveniencing you?" a weak voice asked.

"Just long enough to persuade me to arrange your next stay at Harrod's," she said with a smile.

"What day is it?"

"Monday."

"A long sleep. What happened?"

"You were in the hold when the cargo came free and fell on top of you. You took quite a strike to the head and had Henry Morse earning his keep."

"And you, too, it would seem."

"You need some nourishment. Let me go to the kitchen for something that will help you regain your strength."

"Before you go, tell me one thing: did Asa return home?"

"No."

• • •

October 21, 1774 — Mostly sunny, but cold temperatures brought an early frost. Sam's injuries keep him sore, and a persistent dizziness caused him to remain bedridden until today. He is restless, but the hours we share in conversation seem to relieve the monotony. He is an intellectually curious man who comprehends myriad subjects, and he reads poetry aloud that inspires my mind, body, and soul in ways that I never expected.

Sam dressed slowly, then made his way down the staircase one step at a time. When he reached the kitchen, Dolly was preparing hot oatmeal and smoked fish—hardly gourmet fare, but Sam ate it with the appetite of a bear just awakened from hibernation. With tea in short supply, coffee was the preferred morning beverage; Sam liked its heavy scent and smooth, rich flavor. He came to associate it with Dolly, the femme savior who had nursed him back to health with a staunch determination to oversee his recovery from her home, in spite of the inevitable gossip that would ensue, what with Asa absent from the parsonage.

"It's time for me to get out from underfoot and back into a routine, Dolly. There's too much to be done at the farm, and I suspect that my company is in chaos."

"All in moderation, Sam. Your neighbors tended to your livestock and hayed the field. As for your minutemen, Colonel Rollins has performed the military exercises routinely, if not with your swagger," she teased.

"Well, I need to get moving. I'm afraid the sorrel is in dear need of exercise, so I'll put a saddle on him in the morning and cross the river at Cottle's Ferry. I can follow

Asa's route and see if I can find any signs of him, and I'll venture by the Swans' to see what they know."

"Then I will go with you. There's a sturdy gelding that belongs to the Greenleafs that I occasionally ride, and I'm sure Amy will let me take him for the day."

Sam was not keen on the idea, but why not, he thought. If he had any doubts about Dolly's ability to manage riding horseback in the wilderness, he put them aside. She was more adept at facing challenges than any woman he had ever known, and if he had any physical problems she would be there to tend to them. Plus, he enjoyed her company.

The next morning, Dolly walked to the Greenleafs' stable just after sunrise, saddled the bay gelding, and followed the River Road three miles east to the Dearborn farm. Sam was leading the sorrel from the barn as she arrived.

"You're right on time. Do you want anything before we start out?"

"No, thank you, I've brought along some bread and cheese should we be overcome by hunger. I also have a map and a compass."

"Prepared as always, Mrs. Makepeace," Sam replied with a slight grin.

The ride to Cottle's Ferry was another two miles from Sam's house; there, the river narrowed before sweeping southeasterly through a broad bend.

One of the Cottle boys was there to meet them and greeted Sam with a big smile. "Morning, Captain. Tide's up, so we should have an easy crossing for you. Morning to you, ma'am."

Dolly recognized the boy: his family used to bring him to church at First Parish. Then he'd been kicked in the head by one of the farm animals and had never been quite right again, so he no longer attended Sunday services. He worked the ferry with his mule and made himself useful around the barn and the landing.

"Morning, Willie. Thanks for meeting us."

The boy admired Sam for his military presence and wanted desperately to be a militiaman.

Sam dismounted and helped Dolly do the same. "This is Mrs. Makepeace, the reverend's wife."

Willie tipped his hat in respect. Sam continued, "We believe that Parson Pike may have crossed over here about two weeks ago, and I was wondering if you could confirm that."

"Yessir, I remember. Went across with a mare and chaise. Talked to me about the Baptists and wanted to know why I didn't go to the meetinghouse regular no more. I told him I don't know why we don't go but we ain't no damned Baptists."

"Anyone else I should know about who's crossed here since?"

"No sir, just the usual farmers and woodsmen."

Sam and Dolly led their horses onto the platform and Willie started the old mule around the turnstile, then released the heavy hemp rope, propelling the broad wooden vessel across the Merrimack.

About a third of the way across, Willie suddenly cried out. "Captain, I remember now, there was someone. He came over and back a day or so after."

"Who was it, Willie? Did you recognize him?" Sam hollered.

"Yessir, it was the dandy. The one who lives in the big house across from the village."

The crossing took no more than ten minutes, after which they made their way to a seldom-used trail beyond the banks of the river. They rode single file until a cart path opened the way and the horses were able to proceed side by side.

"What do you suppose Jacob Whooley was doing all the way down here when there's a ferry practically at his front door?" Sam wondered aloud.

Dolly considered the thought before replying. Jacob was a gentleman of high regard, yet he was eccentric, if not downright mysterious, in his habits. No one really knew what he did to occupy his time at the manor house that overlooked the village from Bradford.

"I'm told that Jacob Whooley owns considerable land on this side of the Merrimack."

"He does, but Daniel Swan operates a sawmill east of Johnson's Creek and claims ownership of the land from there to Hawke's meadow. He once cut down an entire orchard of Jacob Whooley's trees because he decided they were on his land."

"Does Jacob contest these encroachments?"

"Until recently, yes, but he dropped a lawsuit to prove his claim to the land. I guess the Swans wore him down so that he had no more stomach to quarrel with them." That seemed odd to Dolly.

"I wonder if the Swan men have some sort of disturbing evidence on Mr. Whooley."

"You mean blackmail?"

"Well, the Swans may be agitators and malcontents, but Jacob Whooley has enough power and influence to put a stop to their mischief any time he so wishes."

Sam considered Dolly's premise in silence as they continued up an incline to an opening in the woods. A small pasture surrounded several ramshackle buildings in the distance.

"Welcome to Swansville," Sam said under his breath. The air was foul and the horses became skittish when two large hogs aggressively charged the split-rail fence that separated their mud-filled pigsty from the gravel path, before retreating and grudgingly allowing the riders passage. A barn and gristmill that straddled a small brook stood opposite the large, run-down cabin that was home to Daniel Swan, his two sons, and several other family members of dubious relation.

Chickens scattered and a dog howled at their approach, while Swan appeared at the doorway. "What's your business here, Dearborn?" he demanded with a rasp. Swan despised Sam. A year earlier, Swan had been accused of stealing a heifer belonging to John Ogden and then intimidating those who might appear against him in a court of law. The evidence was overwhelming: two people had described the heifer's markings as those belonging to a calf that had been delivered in Ogden's meadow the year before, and Sam and Colonel Rollins had stepped forward to mediate the dispute and help the accused recognize his mistake. In the end the beast had been returned to its rightful owner, but the Swan men held grudges and Captain Dearborn would receive no exemption.

"Hello, Daniel, I think you're acquainted with Mrs. Makepeace." Swan ignored the introduction. "We are trying to establish the whereabouts of Asa Pike. He was last known to be circuiting through Bradford from Cottle's Ferry, and I wondered if you happened to see him."

"Came by here about a week or more ago and started in on me for spreading the word of God to my neighbors. I told him I preached the faith of the Lord with the Bible in one hand and a rifle in the other and if he didn't like it I'd be more than glad to show him the way to salvation."

"And how did he respond to such a friendly pastoral debate?"

"With cheek-turning pacifism; he hightailed it out of here just as I reckoned he would."

A wheeze of laughter emanated from the doorway behind, where Robert Swan emerged from the shadows. "Yessir, Captain, he hightailed his rosy cheeks out of here so fast, I thought he'd seen the Holy Ghost himself converting them Baptists."

Amid his laughter, Robert spied Dolly and proffered a conspicuous leer that annoyed Sam. The Swan boys lacked substance and character. Outwardly, Sam displayed considerable tolerance, but inwardly he loathed their crass behavior.

"Have you or your boys seen or heard anything more of Asa Pike since then, Daniel?"

"Timothy," Swan yelled over his shoulder. The youngest Swan emerged from the cabin. "Either of you boys seen or heard anything of the good parson since he passed through here last?"

"No, Pa," they said in near unison.

Sam wondered about the veracity of the information and wanted to question them further, but he was beginning to perspire and Dolly could sense that exhaustion was setting in.

"I think we should be on our way, Captain," she said firmly.

"I expect you can find me in the village if you learn something," Sam shouted as they withdrew. The elder Swan spat on the ground before responding inaudibly.

"Can't say it'd make a bit of difference if I did."

They followed the cart path westerly, veering just enough to the south that the river was no longer in view. Sam was fading quickly, and Dolly realized they had no hope of making it to Bradford and the ferry by sundown and she had no idea where they might take refuge.

"Sam, we need to find someplace to spend the night. It feels like a cold rain, maybe sleet approaching, and you need some rest." Sam gave no argument; he was tired and every bone was starting to ache.

"There's an old fieldstone shelter that was built during the Indian uprisings about a mile south, in the hollow near Johnson's Creek. Not much to look at, but it should do."

Dark clouds moved in rapidly and freezing rain began to soak their clothing. Dolly's fingers were so numb that it was hard to hold the bridle, and the way Sam was hunching over made her fear that he might pass out before they could reach the shelter. On the journey she had not allowed herself to worry much, but now she felt uneasy. There were no familiar landmarks to guide her, so she roused Sam every so often to get him to look about and correct her if she was off course.

A half hour later she found the narrow cutbank that led to the hollow that Sam had described, and crossed over. To her relief, the lodge came into view. It was small, about fifteen feet by eight feet, with a fireplace and chimney at one end. Straw filled a wood-framed loft that served as a bed, to which Dolly guided Sam with a good deal of effort.

Built to withstand Indian raids, the place now served mostly as a shelter for wayfarers or farmers caught in severe weather. Dolly surveyed the room; a tight wooden firkin contained a small supply of grist, and split wood was piled floor to ceiling. By the fireplace were a flint and iron and small amounts of tender. She removed Sam's jacket and waistcoat and got to work to make this cold, drab hut a suitable dwelling. Outside a small lean-to gave the horses cover and feed; she removed their saddles and blankets and settled them for the night.

She broke out the bread and cheese that she carried and sliced small pieces for Sam. He tried a little and drank some cider before falling asleep. As she looked upon him, she judged her companion both patriot and philosopher. Francis Greenleaf had once told her that he had urged Sam to seek admission to Harvard, but Sam had sought out the military instead. Somehow that seemed like the right decision to Dolly. He was strong and charismatic, a natural leader among men. He was devoted to duty, but he weighed the ramifications of his actions with thoughtful deliberation. While he was recovering at the parsonage, she had observed a dimple in his left cheek that appeared with either a smile or a grimace—it did not matter which. It was a feature that broke up an otherwise flawless complexion, yet somehow made him seem more humane.

Humanity was not necessarily a common trait for the men of Haverhill. Dolly's first husband, James Makepeace, had been a pillar of the community, having gained wealth and standing simply because his ancestors were among the founders—proprietors, they were called, the first settlers of the colony and their relatives. In the early days, they had claimed privilege over the control and disposition of all common and undivided lands within the boundaries of Haverhill and profited substantially as a result.

Makepeace had wed Dolly when she was eighteen in a hastily arranged marriage. Her father, Captain John Clarke, was a down-on-his-luck importer of West Indian rum and molasses, when a gale ran three of his ships aground in a setback that threatened to ruin him financially. Dolly loved her father dearly and acquiesced to his proposal to marry Haverhill's prominent merchant if he would guarantee Clarke's losses to his creditors. An agreement was struck and Captain Clarke sailed again, only to drown two years later in the Atlantic. The merchant, who was a strict and jealous husband, had an insatiable appetite for Dolly's gifts that, some believed, brought on the sudden shock that claimed his life. In spite of his proclivity, Dolly bore him no children, but she did inherit his substantial estate, which in her mind was fair consolation.

Suddenly Sam gave a nervous jerk and he started shivering relentlessly. Dolly removed the horse blanket that covered him, then climbed into the loft and wrapped his body around her own. He was cold and pallid. After a while, when his body absorbed her warmth, he responded in short panting breaths. She placed her fingers behind his neck and pressed gently. He had a scent to him like a stable, the smell of horse sweat. It was the scent of desire.

The clouds that had wreaked havoc the night before were stacked threefold in the sky, white fading into blue, by the time Dolly rose the next morning. There was no privy, so she found a suitable spot to relieve herself, then wandered to the creek to wash her hands and face where the water lapped conveniently over a fallen log. She was thinking about Sam and their brief interlude of intimacy and was exploring her feelings, when suddenly she became still. Her intuition had always been keen, and she sensed at this moment that she was being observed. A long shadow stretched slowly from behind, and she pivoted sharply on her heels to discover Robert Swan's gaping grin expelling a frothy mist into the cool morning air.

"You sure are one fine woman," he said with an invasive gaze that spelled trouble.

Dolly made a move to sprint to her left, but Swan's beefy hand pulled her back. She wanted to cry out, but she could see his other hand holding a knife that he could move dexterously from her chin down to her chest. She closed her eyes and felt his earthy breath as he pressed her closer into a repulsive embrace, when there was a *thud*. Her attacker abruptly went limp, then collapsed to the ground in a heap. In his place stood Sam, wielding a heavy branch that had effectively dispatched her nemesis.

"I didn't feel as though I owed him a fair fight," he said with a weary look.

Robert Swan had a headache when he regained his senses, and Dolly gave him a wet washcloth to hold against the bump that was raised on his skull. Sam kept a pistol conspicuous in his waistband and slapped the handle of Swan's hunting knife in his hand as he began his interrogation.

"There are a number of crimes that I could charge you with, Robert, not the least of which is your attempt to assault and defile the wife of our right reverend." Swan began to protest, but Sam cut him off. "Your pa can't get you out of this one, so I suggest you listen to what I have to say and give me some straight answers."

"What can I possibly say that you don't already know?"

"I want you to tell me about your family's land dispute with Jacob Whooley."

"We ain't got no quarrel with Whooley. We settled that whole matter a long time ago."

"Really, what did you promise him to drop his complaint for encroachment?"

"Didn't offer him nothing. He seen the error of his ways."

"That's not good enough, Robert. You know what they do to a man who defiles another man's woman?"

"I didn't defile nobody!"

"Your word against mine." Sam stared him in the eye.

Without his father there to tell him what to do, Robert was helpless and his apprehension was building. He didn't know what they might do to him, but he was frightened by the idea of castration.

"All right, all right, I'll tell you, I will tell you." He paused and closed his eyes to regain his composure before continuing. "We seen Mr. Whooley consorting with the English more than once; why, we even followed him to secret meetings at Shawsheen. Later on he had a whole regiment of Redcoats carting goods to his house. Pa said he was trading information to keep his fancy tastes satisfied."

"And when did you confront Whooley about this discovery?"

"Last month, but we told him we'd keep it a secret as long as he gave up his opposition to our claim on the land."

Sam glanced at Dolly. "All right, Robert, you're free to go, but I don't want you to tell anyone about the events of this morning or of this conversation. Your pa will extend his own brand of punishment if he ever finds out—you can be sure of that."

"No sir, Captain, I won't say a word." With that, Robert slipped back through the woods the way he had come.

"You sure had him anxious," Dolly said.

"Good thing he was alone. Daniel would have called my bluff and given him up."

"Now what?"

"We continue our search for Asa and pay our respects to Jacob Whooley along the way. But first, a little nourishment: I warmed some cornmeal."

"Will you confront him, Sam?" Dolly persisted.

"Who?"

"Jacob."

"No, I don't think that's wise. I'd rather we have a probing conversation with him and take a look around for any corroborating evidence."

The morning drifted away and hardly a word was exchanged as they rode the Salem Post Road through East Bradford. Each was silently recounting the night before, when they had lain side by side, the sound of rain beating on the roof. Some things were best left unspoken, Sam thought, and besides, things had a way of working themselves out. His feelings for Dolly were unmistakable, yet he wasn't entirely certain what part was romance and what was lust.

Dolly was less sanguine. She had married the pastor too soon after James Makepeace's demise. Asa was kind and good company, but he had long ago ceased his appetite for affection without explanation, stranding her in a marriage without passion. She was still the parson's wife and she was fond of Asa, but there would be no way to put a stop to the longing her attraction to Sam was stirring. He was handsome and dashing, but more than that he possessed compassion and strength of character that distinguished him inherently from other men. Last night's closeness confirmed feelings that she could no longer deny.

Long Hill

Dee admired the brilliant late-afternoon foliage as they drove up Long Hill Avenue. You didn't have to go to Vermont, she thought—this was as good a place as any to see the maple and other deciduous trees that burnished the New England landscape in October. She looked down at the old map that she had superimposed over a present-day map of Haverhill using her laptop, and matched up certain landmarks as best she could.

Arthur was navigating his Jeep Cherokee, when Dee asked him to slow down. "Pull over for a minute."

"Here? There's nothing here but a cemetery," Arthur said as he pulled the car to the curb.

"I know, but it looks as though this could lead us to the sinkholes. Drive in and let's see how far we can explore."

An entrance marked "Long Hill Cemetery" led to a series of narrow gravel roads that wound their way around row after row of gravestones on hilly terrain that worked its way down in elevation until the Little River came into view.

"This looks different compared with the old map," Arthur pointed out. "These small bays once visible in the river must have been filled in when the hills between them were leveled. It makes it harder to tell where our sinkholes should be."

"Why don't we take a guess as to the general location and park the Jeep? We can get out and have a look around on foot."

The grounds were not well maintained; autumn leaves amid unmown grass obscured many of the headstones from view. Most of the old graves and mausoleums were from the nineteenth century, but a few seemed older the farther they wandered in the direction of the stream. Arthur looked for any kind of depression that could signal where the mines might once have been.

They were running out of daylight and about to give up, when the feeling returned in Dee: the inner warmth that was both friend and foe. She turned slowly 180 degrees, until something caught her eye.

"Uncle Arthur, come here and have a look at this." An ancient tomb occupied a spot near the corner wall that bordered the cemetery; planted in the ground next to it was a solitary British flag.

"I wonder who placed that here."

Dee examined the granite slab that covered the vault. Moss and lichen blanketed it, but she could feel the work of colonial stonecutters beneath. "There's something engraved here," she said. Arthur produced a pocketknife and carefully peeled back the moss. Protected from the weather by years of benign neglect, the words were still legible: "Unknown Soldiers — 1774."

• • •

Arthur sipped his manhattan as Dee theorized about their discovery.

"It seems unlikely that a British flag was placed there by happenstance," she said. "It seems more likely that someone has knowledge that British soldiers are buried there and honors their memory. We see it with U.S. war casualties all across Europe. Someone must know who this observer is. Do you think the cemetery managers can help us?"

"I doubt it," Arthur replied. "There's been a lot of controversy over the neglect of that cemetery. The city claims no responsibility, and the trustees are unresponsive. There was a young man who was maintaining much of it on his own, and they threw him out for trespassing."

"How can we find out who he is? I'd love to talk to him to see if he knows anything."

"Call the *Gazette*; they covered the story and will give you his name."

Jeremy Murphy was employed at a self-storage facility in one of the old factory buildings that overlooked the Little River, and lived nearby, in the same working-class neighborhood where he had been born and raised. He was a Haverhill High School graduate and an Eagle Scout who took pride in his hometown, and he had felt compelled to improve what he saw as a deplorable situation at the cemetery where most of his family was buried. He worked after hours picking up litter, raking debris, and fixing headstones that were toppled by vandals, until politics and arrogance got in the way. He had embarrassed certain constituencies by drawing attention to the absence of duty to preserve sacred grounds where many of the city's working class had been laid to rest for decades, some even a century or more.

Dee tracked Jeremy down, and he agreed to meet with her at a local coffee shop early the next morning before he reported to work. Since Dee identified herself as a writer, Jeremy thought this was a good chance for more publicity to force improvements to Long Hill Cemetery. It didn't take long for him to figure out that she had a different agenda, but that was all right—he was glad to help.

"I can't help you with the sinkholes. I can see where they were on this map, but I sure haven't ever seen any evidence of them. They could have been filled in years ago at the same time the bays disappeared from view."

Dee was disappointed, but she pressed on to the next question.

"I have another mystery that you might be able to help me with. I stumbled upon an old granite tomb on the grounds. A small British flag had been recently placed before it."

"Down by the wall near the northeast corner," Jeremy said with obvious recognition. "The same old gentleman places it there every year about this time. I don't know his name, but I've seen him at the library. I think he does volunteer work there."

"Lloyd Jones," Arthur said without hesitation as he poured a manhattan. "He taught English literature at Bradford College, a Shakespeare devotee. He spends his time in Special Collections at least three days a week since his retirement. He probably knows as much about

Haverhill and its history as he does about the Bard. He lives in the old Cutter place on Pond Street."

"I would love an introduction, Uncle Arthur. Any knowledge that he has on the unknown soldiers could shed light on this gunpowder incident, not to mention Samuel Dearborn's involvement in whatever defensive actions the town may have mounted. Plus, I would be curious to learn what he knows about Auntie. She seems to have been involved in these events far more than I ever anticipated."

"Well, you've proven to be a pretty tenacious researcher, and Lloyd will appreciate that. I'll call him first thing tomorrow and see if I can arrange for a visit, either at the library or at his home."

October 22, 1774 — Partly sunny, but storm clouds gather in the distance. We have stopped to refresh our horses where Bradford offers a breathtaking view of the valley that greets all who travel the Post Road from Salem. Good tidings portend this final leg of our journey, but I cannot help but wonder what fate has in store for us.

Sam and Dolly rode within sight of the cow common and their horses picked up the pace, somehow sensing that they were near the place where the river separated them from home and stable. The orchard revealed Jacob Whooley's house and soon they were in a full gallop that exhilarated Dolly, before Sam reined in the sorrel and the bay gelding followed suit. Thunder rumbled in the distance as they pulled up behind the English Tudor–style stable. Jacob spied them from the stalls and greeted them as he closed the barn door behind him.

"Captain Dearborn and Mrs. Makepeace, what a splendid surprise. Welcome to Whooley Manor."

"We seem to have outrun the rain, Jacob. May we stable our horses?"

"Of course you may, Captain, but leave them right there for Ned; he will brush them down and tend to their care. Please come inside."

Ned had been born a slave, and though Jacob's father had granted him his freedom, he was generally indentured to a life of servitude to Jacob. They had been raised together at Whooley Manor and Ned was completely loyal to Jacob, even though he judged Jacob's lifestyle unfavorably. His mother had kept him too close, Ned was sure. Now he oversaw the grounds and his wife, Jewel, managed the household with complete discretion. Sam knew Ned slightly and had high regard for his steadfastness; he had once even tried to recruit him to his company of minutemen.

"Hello, Ned. How's Jewel?"

"She's fine, Captain, thank you for asking. You'll find her for yourself in the pantry."

Inside, Jewel served refreshments while Jacob asked about their journey. "You have traveled a great distance on horseback, Mrs. Makepeace. I am astonished by your resilience. Some of the tomboy in you must have survived adolescence."

"A good horse is worth more than riches, as the saying goes, Mr. Whooley, and the Greenleafs' gelding is an easy ride."

"And you, Captain, what are the purpose and result of your investigation?"

"We're searching for Asa Pike. He's been missing for almost a fortnight with no word and only one sighting, by the Swans. We fear that he might have suffered an accident or encountered highwaymen, but we can find no such evidence."

"Oh? What did the Swan ruffians have to report?"

"Just that he passed through. However, they warned us about reports of British riders, which I found troubling."

"More rumors," Jacob said dismissively. "Perhaps Parson Pike went on to Rowley; there are more than a few Baptists preaching over there."

"Perhaps, but that is another day's ride, and unless we have good reason to suspect that he is there, we really must return to the village. By the way, do you still own that tract of forest leading up to Johnson's Creek?"

The question caught Whooley off guard. "It's, ah, tied up in negotiations. Why do you ask?"

"Well, the Swan men act as though they own it, and I could see where they have clear-cut some timber. Seems like more mischief."

"Really. I'll have to look into that." An hour passed amiably, before Whooley asked Ned to ready his guests' horses. As they waited, Dolly and Sam wandered through Jacob's fall garden.

"I think Asa has been here and Jacob is hiding information from us, Sam."

Sam raised his brow inquiringly.

Dolly continued, "Only Asa could have revealed to him my tomboy days, and how does he know that Asa's mission was to seek out itinerant preachers?"

"I'd like to get a look inside the stable," Sam replied. "Why don't you ask Jacob for a guided tour of the manor house before we leave?"

Jacob was flattered by the suggestion and took Dolly by the arm, pointing out the carved family crests and medieval antiquities that adorned the hallways and gathering rooms.

Sam slipped quietly out the back door and made a beeline for the stable. He entered the small door through the tack room, then made his way to the horse stalls. As he entered, Ned stood with his back to Sam, bridling the sorrel. The gelding was already saddled and was nosing up to another horse in the stall immediately opposite. Sam took a closer look: it was Asa's gray mare.

"All right, Ned, I need some answers," he said quietly, yet quite enough to startle him.

Asa looked up from his book when Jacob entered the room on the second floor.

"We have been discovered and found guilty of deception," Jacob said laconically. Behind him, Sam and Dolly stared in with disbelief. Here was Asa Pike, relaxed and seemingly free to move about as he pleased, while they had been searching the countryside for the better part of two days.

"I guess we have some explaining to do," Asa understated. Asa and Jacob talked late into the afternoon describing the events that had led to Jacob's coercement by lieutenant Hannibal Jones, Bart Preble's murder, and the manifestation of Asa's renaissance and commitment to his subjugator and host.

Dolly was still reeling from the revelations when Ned burst into the room.

"Mr. Whooley, British soldiers are coming down our road."

"This way, Captain." Jacob pulled on the red leather–bound volume that released the secret entrance to the cavern below.

"Ned," Sam called back, "the horses." Ned gave a knowing nod, then ran from the library through the kitchen and outdoors.

The Englishman

Lloyd Jones was an Englishman in most every way. His neatly trimmed mustache blended nicely with his warm smile, and he greeted guests with an engaging accent that suggested peerage. He wore a four-in-hand tie even when relaxing at home in his cardigan sweater, and he would announce to anyone who asked about the collarless knitted jacket that it was named for the Seventh Earl of Cardigan, a British cavalryman of Crimean War fame. Dee admired the two-story Greek Revival, with its four columns and pediment facing Pond Street. This was the mansion where Dr. Jones often invited students, faculty, and friends to engage in academic debate during his tenure as the distinguished professor of English literature at Bradford College. On this night he welcomed Arthur Dearborn's niece from Michigan.

"So, your uncle tells me that you are doing some genealogy and you are interested in the history of our town."

"Well, not really genealogy, Dr. Jones. I'm actually interested in learning all that I can about the lives of one specific generation of my family during the period leading up to the Revolution."

"Of course you mean the Rebellion," he said with a wry expression.

Dee smiled. "Yes, Dr. Jones, the Rebellion. One of my ancestors seven generations ago was the commander of the local minutemen. I think he may have been involved in a skirmish with the British that occurred in October 1774, over a gunpowder operation that may have been centered in Haverhill."

"That's six months before Lexington and Concord, Miss Dearborn. Surely history would not have overlooked such an episode without some record of its having taken place."

"Well, that's the puzzle," Dee said. "I have found mention of a confrontation, but there is no military record that I can find to back it up."

"And what is the source for your thesis?"

"Well, I have been using the HPL online database, and I have been to the New England Historical Society on several—"

Jones interrupted politely. "No, no. I mean, what are your *primary* sources?"

Dee paused before answering. "I have a diary," she said bluntly but confidently.

"A diary? What kind of a diary?" Jones interrogated.

"It's a diary that belonged to my ancestor Dolly Makepeace. She was the wife of captain Samuel Dearborn."

"What does the diary reveal that has led you to my door?"

"It reveals nothing directly, but it creates a spiritual experience—a sixth sense that led me to a grave of unknown soldiers on Long Hill. You placed a small British flag there to honor these men."

"And all this is written in the diary?"

"No. Just the clues that directed us there."

"And how can you be sure of its authenticity without corroborating supportive data?"

"It came from my ancestral home, where it remained hidden away for years. Dolly Makepeace recorded these events in her diary as historical fact. I can tell it is authentic and I know it is the truth," she said, a bit defensively.

Jones challenged her: "And how can you know that, young lady? In fact, other than a gravestone, how can you prove this woman ever existed?"

"Because I have a sensation inside me that tells me when she is near—a glow that expresses a calling that only I can hear, because it's . . . " Now her eyes were welling up with tears.

"A glow that grasps your inner soul, a glow that speaks to you from beyond, a glow that you cannot turn on or off at will," Jones said with an expression of sadness and relief.

"Yes, exactly. How do you know that?" she asked.

"Because, Miss Dearborn, we both have a gift: it is called retrocognition. You have knowledge of past events that cannot be learned through normal means of study. We share this rare psychic experience, but your senses are far more acute than mine. You perceive subtle dimensions of the unseen universe of our ancestors that I can only rationalize, since they are beyond my reach. Indeed, you possess a degree of clairvoyance, which your ancestor has awakened, that I envy. I had to test you to be sure, Miss

Dearborn. But together we can channel these powers to a new level of discovery."

"Can this gift lead me to the answers that I am searching for about my ancestor Dolly Makepeace?"

"The answer to that question depends on an investigation around the cemetery and our mysterious tomb. We won't know unless we try."

The next day Dee called Jeremy Murphy and asked him to meet her, and explained that she was looking for clues about the existence of the sinkholes. Arthur and Lloyd Jones were already at the cemetery when they arrived, and Dolly made the introductions. The party was assembled for a broad inspection of the grounds surrounding the tomb. Arthur paced the perimeter near the stone wall while the professor adjusted a handheld GPS. Suddenly, Jones stopped in his tracks and looked up with a puzzled expression.

"I have checked the coordinates twice, and this device tells me that this should be the exact position of the sinkholes. That means the entrance must be nearby. After all these years, could it have been right under my nose?" Jones sat on the tomb and looked around for clues. Suddenly, he began waving his arms and shouting. "The tomb, the tomb! The coordinate converter map points right here. It must be within the tomb." The others jogged over and gathered around.

"Let's remove the slab and have a look," Dee said.

Jeremy grabbed one end and Dee helped Arthur with the other. It was heavier than expected, but they successfully lifted it, then eased it on its side against the vault. They peered into the compartment in silence: empty—no remains. Instead, at one end a death head with wings was carved into the stone pedestal.

Arthur reached in with his pocketknife. There was a faint square border around the pattern; he cleared away centuries of dust, until a small handhold became visible. He tried pulling, to no avail. "Jeremy, you give it a shot."

Jeremy pulled hard with his muscular frame until a trapdoor gradually opened onto a space of unknown proportion. A rush of dank, stale air escaped into the atmosphere.

"Do you feel it, Miss Dearborn?" Jones asked.

"Yes, I can definitely feel some kind of energy. It is stronger than anything I have experienced before."

October 22, 1774, cont. — The world turned upside down. Asa has found himself a new life that I will never be able to explain to his congregation, whilst British soldiers have taken positions across the river from our town. We must find an escape from beneath the earth, where we are far from heaven and, I pray, not on some path to purgatory.

Sam was cursing himself. He regretted ever having thought about bringing Dolly along and exposing her to such danger, especially when he knew he was not fit enough to protect her. What was he thinking? It was bad enough that Robert Swan had tried to force himself on her at the stone cabin, but now he had led her into an ambush set by a ruthless Redcoat who had already murdered Bart Preble and would gladly kill again to keep his intentions secret.

He should have sent her back after the unfriendly encounter with the Swans, he thought. Cottle's Ferry was only a few miles away, and Willie would surely have seen her and brought her back. Then she could have backtracked to the farm and would have been home by nightfall. But Sam had been consumed by his own desires and wanted Dolly's company. Now they were trapped and he would have to figure a way out to see her safely home.

Sam's eyes measured the boundaries of the wine cellar. He could see no other passages, but the flame in the lantern was attracted to the northwest corner, for some reason, so he thought he should take a closer look.

"Dolly, over here," he whispered.

A narrow passage led to what he was hoping for: a smaller cavern in which they could hide and even explore as far as it would take them. Sam lifted his lantern for a better view: more barrels, but not rum barrels this time.

"These are dry-tight casks," he said to Dolly. "Thirty-six missing gunpowder kegs, stolen and hidden here by Bart Preble." But how? he wondered. There had to be a subterranean means of access.

Sam remembered Dolly's compass. "Let's follow this passage northwest and see where it takes us."

The tunnel was pitch dark for some distance, before they crawled through an opening that led to an enormous cavern. Stalagmites reached upward from the floor of the grotto, and corresponding stalactites hung downward from a flat ceiling. The light from the lantern reflected softly off the columns, giving off a warm glow and revealing an underground waterway that mirrored the colorful formations. The surrounding natural beauty entranced Dolly. It was like a room belonging to angels, she thought.

She was nearly spellbound when noises from the rear interrupted the tranquility: the British were on their trail.

She shouted a warning, but Sam was already on the alert. He spied a long, flat-bottomed pram at the edge of the water—Bart's cargo vessel, no doubt. He helped Dolly climb in; then they pushed off, pulling the oars silently through the crystal-clear pool.

Hannibal Jones and Corporal Daggett followed the passage Sam and Dolly had taken. The Recoats had discovered their horses before Ned could hide them, and the officer was determined to hunt down and eliminate whoever threatened to reveal the British presence. Aboveground, sixteen grenadiers positioned four cannons on the high ground of Jacob Whooley's manor house. General Gage had ordered the clandestine raid in order to seek out and destroy the rogue gunpowder facilities, and Jones was prepared to lay a surprise siege upon the village and gain the general's favor at all cost.

As he entered the subterranean cavern, Jones noticed ripples in the pool that led the way to a labyrinth of passages. He looked along the shoreline for any means of pursuit. As his eyes adjusted to the light, he spied a small punt in the shadows that would accommodate them. Daggett grabbed a pole, and they began navigating the underground aqueduct.

Although the waterway stretched underground for what seemed a great distance, there did not seem to be much of a current, just acres of pristine water. Sam and Dolly thought they could hear voices in the distance, so they pressed ahead in silence. A small landing appeared where the passage narrowed. Sam looked at the compass. Given the time and direction, he suspected they were somewhere beneath the West Parish by now, and he motioned for Dolly to disembark.

"There has to be another passageway to the sinkholes," he whispered. "It's the only way that Bart could have moved so much gunpowder efficiently. Let's follow this tunnel."

After about five minutes, a dome pit intersected the left wall of the passage. Inside were three more portals. The one to the left was muddy, while the center one was tight and an unlikely passage as a smugglers' tunnel. The one to the right, however, was of walking dimensions, so they navigated it for no more than a minute before arriving at a small cavern room about twenty feet in diameter. Here they could rest.

Aboveground and unbeknownst to Lieutenant Jones, his grenadiers, left unattended, had invaded the wine cellar and proceeded to drink the rum and other spirits that were stored alongside Whooley's wine collection. As their intoxication increased, so did their attentions diminish, allowing Jacob and Asa to escape their predicament, along with Ned and Jewel.

The Crypt

Professor Jones advocated that they reseal the tomb before beginning any kind of exploration. Permission would be necessary before they could enter such a historic grave.

"I will arrange for a permit from the Department of Archaeology and Historic Preservation," he explained at dinner that evening. "In the meantime, I would like Miss Dearborn to accompany me to the parapsychology department at the college. A crash course in the methodology used in such investigations would be useful."

"What can I do?" Arthur asked.

"I would ask that you drive to Salem first thing tomorrow. The Peabody Essex Museum is photocopying several historic maps that will be helpful to us."

The next morning, Arthur switched on the windshield wipers to high in the Jeep. Torrentially rainy weather had returned overnight, and some roads were experiencing flooding. He stopped at the coffee shop and picked up Jeremy, who would act as his guide through any alternate routes to Salem. Jeremy was not much of a conversationalist, so when he spoke up it was usually because he had something relevant to say.

"I don't mean to second-guess the professor, but I don't know why he needs a permit from anyone other than the cemetery. Why, people here enter those old mausoleums all the time to make repairs or even to do genealogical investigations. As long as you can prove that you're not disturbing the dead, you're okay, and since we already proved that it's empty, I don't see the need. It's not like we're involved in some archaeological dig."

Arthur mulled that thought over in his head. It would surely save them some time if the permitting process could be shortened.

"Let me see if I can reach Dee." Arthur dialed her cell phone, but the call went directly to her voicemail. "Well then, let's see if we can track down the professor." He pressed 411, asked for the college, and was quickly connected.

"Bradford College," came the voice at the other end.

"Department of parapsychology, please."

"I'm sorry. What department?"

"Parapsychology," he repeated slowly.

"I'm sorry, sir, we have no such department at Bradford College."

Professor Jones pulled into Arthur Dearborn's driveway, and Dee emerged from the house with a cup of coffee in hand and climbed into the Range Rover.

"Good morning," she said. "I probably shouldn't be drinking coffee; I have enough jitters as it is."

Jones ignored the greeting. "I thought we should go by the cemetery first. If you have any postcognitive impulses, it would be good to have them fresh in your subconscious when we meet the clinicians at Bradford."

Dee thought this unnecessary, but she did not object. The road up Long Hill Avenue was slippery with wet leaves, and the SUV lurched as its wheels spun, then regained traction. Something in the trunk fell over with a *clank*.

"What was that?" Dee asked.

"It's a pneumatic device that we will employ to remove the slab from the tomb."

"Why are we doing that? I thought we needed a permit."

"I have decided to circumvent the process. You and I can expedite this investigation if we make this exploration alone."

"I don't think I really want to do that, Professor Jones. Please, let's proceed to the college and wait for my uncle to return with the maps."

"The die is cast, Miss Dearborn—our ancestors await our appearance." Jones pulled into the cemetery and removed a pistol from the pocket of his jacket.

"Whoa! What is this all about?"

"It is about salvation, Miss Dearborn. It is about family honor. It is about changing the outcome of one forgotten historical event that will restore the good name and reputation of lieutenant Hannibal Jones and deliver him to his rightful place among England's esteemed military leaders. Now let's get moving."

A simple aluminum tripod connected to a compressed air hoist easily removed the heavy slab from the grave. Dee followed Jones's instructions and affixed a clamp to the handhold within, then slowly exerted just enough power to reopen the trapdoor. Jones aimed his flashlight into the cavity to reveal a brick and mortar–lined tunnel just large enough to pass through single file.

"All right, Miss Dearborn, you first."

Dee thought about refusing, but her curiosity and sixth sense had the best of her, and she wanted to engage whatever it was that was within the old crypt. She lowered herself feet first into the darkness, then assisted the professor as he followed her into the passage.

The air was heavy with dust as they walked with stooped posture through the centuries-old tunnel. Several minutes later, Jones's lamp revealed the date 1775 engraved in one wall. Here the brickwork ended, and they continued down a declining passage that led to an alcove where they could rest and get their bearings.

"How far do you think these passages go?" Dee asked.

"This I cannot foretell. These caverns were created millions of years ago, most likely during the Cretaceous period, and the passageways to such natural formations are always varied and unpredictable."

"How long have you known of their existence?"

"It was not until I became aware of your paranormal presence. The grave was always a force, a place where I could communicate, but I never knew of the sinkholes. I knew only that my ancestor was the victim of some terrible misfortune that occurred during a clandestine, and therefore unrecorded, raid on Haverhill. General Gage would not admit to the affair, and so Lieutenant Jones suffered an ignominious fate, buried in an unmarked tomb. This injustice has been passed down from generation to generation of family members, but I am the first to actively seek any measure of redress and vindication."

"We are 236 years removed, Professor Jones. Why don't you just write a paper and submit it to the Historical Society?"

"Because that is not enough!" he shouted, before regaining his composure. "You see, Miss Dearborn, I believe that through telekinesis you and I can change the outcome of events—turn back the clock, so to speak, and alter history."

"And what event will you try to change?"

"The confrontation and death struggle between Hannibal Jones and Samuel Dearborn."

"How do you know such a conflict took place?"

"Through research, family lore, and clairvoyance. I have visualized it many times, my dear. Now I know where it occurred: here within this subterranean labyrinth, during an effort to seize and destroy Haverhill's gunpowder operation."

"But how can you hope to change what has already happened?"

"By eliminating Captain Dearborn," he said coolly. Dee was stunned. Did the old professor really believe that he had the power to thrust himself into an event that had occurred two centuries earlier? The idea was preposterous, yet if he did alter just one event, he could change dramatically, the course of history. The professor interrupted her reverie. "Let's keep moving, young lady."

Fire in the Hole

A succession of loud reports echoed through the cavern and startled even Hannibal Jones. The shots came from the rear, he was certain, but he had given orders that his grenadiers should not commence any acts of aggression until he returned. Could they have found themselves under attack from the Americans?

He looked at Daggett and spoke decisively. "Let us catch these renegades and dispatch them quickly." They removed their flintlock pistols and cocked them for action.

Sam was fading fast—the exertion had taken its toll on him physically—but Dolly kept urging him on. They heard the gunshots and were certain that the Redcoats were onto them, though how many, they did not know.

"Come on!" Dolly cried out. "There's an incline ahead and I can feel a change in the air."

"You go ahead, Dolly. I'll stay here and take my best shot."

"Then I'm staying, too."

"Are you crazy?"

"Of course—I'm with you, am I not?"

"You most certainly are not going to—"

"Then you had better come with me; one lead ball from your pistol won't stop the entire British army."

He would go with her. Their perilous flight had brought him to the realization that he loved her, and besides, things had a way of working out. Just ahead was another alcove where they could take cover. Jones and Daggett were close on their heels, and Sam thought he could see silhouettes in the near distance. At the opening he drew his pistol as a precaution; then a sudden static flash filled the air and blinded them momentarily. Sam blinked to regain his vision. Before them stood Jones and Daggett with arms extended and flintlock pistols in hand.

"Captain Dearborn, I presume, and Mrs. Makepeace." Sam knew they were in a dire predicament and concealed his sidearm.

"You have our surrender, Lieutenant."

"Ah, but your crime is treason, and the penalty is far more severe. I am truly sorry to be the cause of your flight from all earthly joys, yet a more eternal rest awaits, I am certain."

Sam reacted and fired the pistol, sending a shot that glanced the sleeve of Corporal Daggett's tunic. Now the Redcoats took aim and fired at point-blank range. Nothing. Their powder, dampened by the high moisture content or perhaps by flints too wet to spark, would not ignite the charge. Jones threw the pistol aside and reached for his short saber, when another flash of static filled the limestone room.

• • •

The alcove into which Professor Jones and Dee Dearborn had ultimately descended had suddenly come alive, and the struggle between Sam, Dolly, and the Redcoats was playing out right before their astonished eyes. Sam's errant shot and the misfires of the pistols all happened in what seemed an instant, and Lloyd Jones knew that this was his time. The drama that he had rehearsed in his head for decades was about to unfold. He raised the .38 caliber pistol and took dead aim at Captain Dearborn.

"Stop thy unhallowed toil, vile Montague! Can vengeance be pursued further than death? Condemned villain, I do apprehend thee; for thou must die."

"No!" Dee shouted, shoving the professor forcefully. The firearm discharged and a report echoed off the cavern walls. The British officer seemed disoriented and staggered for a few steps. He put his hand to his chest and stared at the old man in disbelief—mortality was incomprehensible, yet the bullet had found its destination in the breast of Hannibal Jones's red tunic. Corporal Daggett hurried down the passageway and disappeared into eternal darkness.

Dee had fallen to the hard floor of the cave.

"Ow," she complained loudly.

"Are you hurt?" a voice asked. She examined the abrasions on her elbows, then looked upward. Dolly Makepeace, whose face expressed a balance of strength and compassion, fixed her eyes on her counterpart with familial empathy.

"Auntie?"

• • •

Aboveground, Robert Swan had been unable to keep the clash with Sam a secret from his father, and Daniel was furious that someone had dared administer a beating to one of his sons, much less coerce a confession from him concerning the Whooley land scheme. He gathered the Swan men, including two sons-in-law, and they rode hard by horseback to the manor house, where he intended to catch up to the high-and-mighty Captain Dearborn and extract his measure of revenge. Instead, when they arrived they surprised an inebriated regiment of British soldiers, who found themselves face-to-face with the posse of filthy, angry woodsmen. If Hannibal Jones had been present, or even Corporal Daggett, a confrontation probably could have been avoided, but when one of the grenadiers raised his rifle in a panic, Timothy Swan heaved his hunting knife with deadly precision.

All hell broke loose. Shots were fired and horses reared and spun about in confusion as the Swan men sprinted for cover. Musket balls flew back and forth for a good twenty minutes, and, though outnumbered by their rivals three to one, the frontiersmen were rapidly cutting down the drunk and leaderless soldiers. In desperation, a grenadier remembered the cannon placements and ran to where one was loaded and ready at an elevated position overlooking the village. As the Swans advanced, he pivoted the cannon 180 degrees before igniting the fuse. The ensuing blast sent a cannonball at a low trajectory directly into the side of the house, tearing away a whole portion of the east wall and creating a gaping hole.

Moments later, in a delayed reaction, an enormous explosion sent a geyser of flames through the roof and high into the air, signaling that the explosive ball had found its way to Bart Preble's hidden magazine. Inside the cellar, thirty-six kegs of black powder and countless bottles of wine ignited, sending a backdraft of fire and toxic fumes rushing through the passages that lay beneath the Merrimack and toward the West Parish and the sinkholes.

Dolly guided Sam through a portal as a push of warm, ashen air began its suffocating escape from below. The natural shaft continued up at a slight grade, before revealing a small cavern at the second sinkhole, which had been left largely unexplored. A dark, forbidding place, it was home to thousands of bats. Clusters of them clung to the walls and ceiling overhead, flying mammals of prey and omens of superstition that people avoided. Now they were agitated and swept about in frightening chaos, before forming a vortex that led to the cave egress and the sloping meadow of Long Hill. A lethal cloud of gaseous smoke followed them out of the ground, like a chimney flue. Dolly and Sam stumbled out for several paces, then supported each other as their gaze was drawn unavoidably toward the distant Merrimack.

The southern sky was a soft orange pastel, illuminated by a pandemonium of flames that reached high into the night above Whooley Manor. They stared in silence, until Sam put his arms around Dolly and kissed her fervently; after all, he was her man and he knew that she loved him.

The Pediment

Arthur and Jeremy sped up Long Hill Avenue in the worst rainstorm to hit Merrimack Valley in years. Rivers and streams had not yet crested, but when they did, many underground passages would surely flood. They pulled up in a hurry next to Lloyd Jones's Range Rover, then ran to the open tomb.

"Dee! Dee!" Arthur yelled into the darkness. "I'm going in."

"Wait a second, I hear something," Jeremy hollered. Voices from within the tunnel echoed beneath the drum of the driving rain. Jeremy pointed his flashlight into the abyss. One human form, then another, began to emerge from below the trapdoor in the pedestal. Jeremy assisted a visibly shaken Lloyd Jones to the surface; then Arthur reached down and pulled Dee into the murky daylight.

"Are you all right?"

Dee nodded her head but did not speak; she was either shaking from the ordeal or shivering from the cold. Arthur could not be sure which, but he threw his jacket over her shoulders and guided her to the car. Jeremy helped Professor Jones into the Range Rover and headed for the Pond Street residence, where they agreed to rendezvous and debrief.

On the ride over, Dee gave Arthur the ten-minute version of the day's events, including Jones's discharge of the pistol in the cavern hundreds of feet beneath the cemetery but leaving out any mention of the apparition.

"I should have called the police," Arthur said with a fury in his voice.

"Don't do that, Uncle Arthur. I don't think Dr. Jones meant to harm me."

"You could have been killed down there. There are flood warnings, and that idiot old man takes you down into a cave chasing ghosts with a loaded gun! He should have his head examined."

"He's not crazy. Let him go home; he's had enough excitement for one day."

Professor Jones was sullen yet contrite, hardly the man who had entertained his guests so confidently the night before. He had manipulated his friend's niece, only to realize the fatal flaw of his delusional scheme. The character of this Jones line of Englishmen had been ignobly exposed.

Yet they had achieved a great breakthrough, he and the young Dearborn woman. Indeed, he thought, somehow he must redeem himself in her eyes.

By the time Dee and Arthur arrived, Jeremy had a fire going in the library and Jones was warming up in body and in spirit.

"I apologize to you, young lady," he pleaded over a cup of tea. "I had no intention of endangering you, and I only now appreciate the strength of your devotion to the estimable Dolly Makepeace. You are to be admired for your fidelity to someone who possessed such virtue, determination, and remarkable beauty, so fair of face."

"Thank you for your apology, Professor Jones. I realize now that we share not only an unusual psychological gift but also exceptional ancestral histories that intersected for better or worse more than two hundred years ago. Yet I beg to ask: your description of Dolly Makepeace was beautifully spoken, but how did you come to envision her so poignantly?"

"Aha, that is my final surprise. Come with me, my dear, and you too, gentlemen." Jones became animated as they walked through the parlor to the staircase. "James Cutter was in the shoe-manufacturing business and a man of some distinction when he built this house in 1908. At the time, the parsonage, which had endured for so many years, was being demolished in the name of progress to make room for a new high school. Mr. Cutter very much admired the columns and pediment that had given the building its stately appearance, and so he had them removed and added to the design of his new house."

Arthur looked out the second-floor window at the four Ionic columns before climbing the stairs to the third floor.

"You may have noticed the pediment has a small oval window below the apex. There are narrow built-in storage pockets on either side just big enough for a card table, and that's exactly what this one was used for," Jones said, pointing to the thin beveled door on the left as they alighted on the third-floor landing. "When I opened this one, however, I discovered something far more interesting."

Jones unlatched the matching door to the right. Inside was a large square object draped in an old wool blanket.

Jones carefully slid it out and slowly removed the cover. At first sight, Dee was breathtaken. A modest antique gilded frame bordered an oil painting of a woman with a precise smile, handsome and noble yet without pretense—indisputably American.

"It's Aunt Dolly," she said, without having to be told. She stared at the portrait in silence for a long, satisfying moment, when her eye caught something in the lower-right-hand corner. "P. Gallimet," she said in a near whisper. "The Frenchman really was an artist."

October 27, 1774 — Five days have passed since the ordeal. I try to make sense of events that have changed my life forever. Asa and Jacob have vanished, and the townspeople say that they perished in the inferno that destroyed Whooley Manor. Perhaps, but I would sooner believe that they have found a new place where their souls are joined in cheerful bliss. For now I will remain at the parsonage, at least until a new minister is found. As for Sam Dearborn, he is now an inseparable part of my life. I know not how or when, but I will take him as my husband. The stars and planets are in alignment.

Sixteen British soldiers were dead or missing—most buried where they fell, two of them interred somewhere beneath Long Hill. Colonel Rollins ordered that the entrances to the sinkholes be filled, and a cleverly constructed access was disguised as an anonymous grave to keep their continued existence a secret. General Gage, upon learning of the debacle, assumed that the explosion was the result of the catastrophic destruction of the powder-manufacturing operation but disavowed any knowledge of the politically sensitive operation.

As for the Swan men, they never knew what hit them. The concussion from the blast was so severe that anyone within a hundred feet was killed instantly. They were given Christian burials in the town cemetery.

Ned and Jewel were rumored to have moved to St. John's Island in Canada, where many loyalist refugees fled in the years surrounding the Revolution. They found a piece of land, which they purchased through the generosity of an unknown benefactor, farming it in the summer and fishing in the winter months. They prospered and raised five children.

On the morning of November 7, 1774, Jacob Whooley and Asa Pike stood on the deck of the British brig *Hope* as the Tory ship departed Boston Harbor for England. Whatever emotion they held in their hearts, they knew that they had little choice but to leave America and start a new life together in Yorkshire. The Whooley family would perceive Jacob's return to the mother country as an act of loyal sacrifice and had promised the men a small manor house.

The brig was doing an easy six knots before a freshening breeze as they gathered in their last view of Cape Ann and the harbor entrance to the Merrimack.

"What say you, sir?" Jacob asked his pensive partner.

"This is a grand country we are departing, Jacob, a place where hard work and an honest heart can take one a great distance. We leave behind many friends and family whose loss I shall grieve, none more so than my companion and wife, whom I adore and now set free. May God speed you on life's journey, Dolly Makepeace."

— THE END —

About the Author

Arthur Hale Veasey III was born and raised in Haverhill, Massachusetts. He was educated at Governor Dummer Academy in nearby Byfield, Massachusetts before completing his higher education at the University of Denver in Colorado. The Diary of Dolly Makepeace is his first novel. Mr. Veasey also writes short stories and has contributed essays to numerous publications. He presently resides in West Newbury, Massachusetts with his wife and two children.

Made in the USA
Lexington, KY
21 January 2013